The Travel Club

BOOK ONE

Jeanie Wood

© Jeanie Wood 2022

ISBN: 978-0-6455546-0-1

All rights reserved. Except for private study, criticism or reviews, as permitted under the Copyright Act, no part of this book may be reproduced, stored in a retrieval system, or transmitted in any form or by any means without prior written permission. Enquiries should be forwarded to the publisher.

Cataloguing in Publications entry is available from the National Library of Australia http:/catalogue.nla.gov.au

Publisher's note: This novel is a work of fiction. Names, characters, places and incidents are either products of the author's imagination or used fictitiously. All characters are fictional, any similarity to people living or dead is purely coincidental.

First edition published 2019 by Elephant House Press

Second edition published 2022 by Wood Words

COVER DESIGN BY JEANIE WOOD AND AMBER BOLTON. © Jeanie Wood 2022

With thanks to Kelly Wood, Adele Lockman and others for advice. Special thanks to the ladies of the Castle Hill and District Probus Club Choir for their great silhouettes.

L. WOOD WORDS ▬▶

DEDICATION

For my darling husband Lyall, with whom, hand in
hand, I have trodden many foreign shores –
both literally and figuratively.

ACKNOWLEDGMENTS

The author would like to thank:

Elizabeth Chapman from Elephant House Press, editor and encourager who read my story and transformed it into this book's first incarnation.

My darling husband Lyall: friend, encourager, comforter and my other half. Thank you for your unwavering support.

My readers: my dear daughter-in-law Kelly Wood who has constantly supported my writing and made it feel of value and my son Peter Wood who gave me great advice on how a young man would feel and speak. The rest of my family who encourage my work as an author.

The Omega Writers' Group, without whose inspiration this would have never been written.

And last but not least, thanks to God for this great adventure.

There are times, moments, nanoseconds, if you like, when our world stands still, and reality takes a magnetic shift like our poles are reversed.

Sometimes it happens slowly – like a wall of water far out at sea, creeping towards you until everything you know is transformed.

And sometimes it happens in a blink.

Jeanie Wood

PART 1 - THE JOURNEY

CHAPTER ONE

'She's back,' the girl puckered her dark lips in what his mother had described as 'pussy-bum-face' and stared through the shop front, 'AND she's talking to somebody.'

It crossed Peter's mind that it was a free world. Well, maybe not free when it came to travelling places – that cost a lot. And all the posters of exotic places were supposed to whet your appetite – make you spend money. Mind you, most people either came into the travel agency, or moved on. Not many bought a cup of coffee and stood transfixed in the front of the window as if they were at the movies.

He turned his head away from the hot glare of the computer screen and contemplated the two women in front of the store.

'I'm going to ask if I can help her.' Kath or Kathy or Katy or whatever she wanted to be called today was rising off her wheelie chair, her mouth set like a brick wall, heading for the door.

'Leave her alone.'

She paused mid lunge, hand extended to the door handle like a stick figure. 'But she'll scare off other customers.'

'She's an old woman, not a monster.' He turned back to the

screen.

'She's blocking the window.'

'What from? There's nobody else about.' He wished she would stop talking and leave him – and the woman – alone.

'She's scary.'

'Wearing her balaclava today, is she?'

'No.' She sniffed.

'Her eyes are bright red?'

'I can't see them behind her glasses.' Katy dropped her arm and turned back to her desk

'It must be the broomstick. Go and remind her to park it in the parking lot.'

'Hmph, you'll be sorry.' She added, 'You'll see.'

He glanced sideways, then muttered, 'She reminds me of my mother.'

Anna knew it wasn't right to stare in the travel agent's window all the time. She knew it upset the young dolly-girl inside, and she cared about that even less than she cared about what she wore. Living in the units surrounding the mall, she spent uncounted hours shuffling around, staring in the windows of shops at things she would never be able to afford and didn't really need. At least it was warm in here.

More and more she found herself retreating into her memories, the present had become unreal, pressing but passing.

The pictures on the travel agent's glass shopfront drew her in. Was that scent of fresh cake from the coffee shop further down the corridor or was she in the Ringstrasse in Vienna outside her favourite café? She could scarcely tell. How long had she been immersed in that poster when the woman spoke to her? Anna didn't hear the first few words and turned with a creased brow.

'Isn't it beautiful,' the stranger was saying, 'we had such a lovely time in Vienna.' Anna turned to move away but the stranger gripped her arm, halting her flight. 'Have you been there?' the woman asked.

Anna gazed at the hand. It was wrinkled and gnarled around the finger joints, like an aged tree limb, and the veins on the back stood out like forked branches. She was mentally comparing her own weathered hands to the one gripping her. Looking up into the stranger's face she saw tears gathering along the lower rim of the eyes, then they were blinked away as the woman regained control.

'We were happy there.' The woman suddenly released her arm.

Anna nodded. All those years ago, she had also been happy there. 'It was a beautiful place.' Her voice croaked. Their gaze turned once again to the poster. Embarrassment hung in the air like the mists of time.

The stranger once again extended her hand and said, 'Come and have coffee with me and let's talk about Vienna.'

And, surprising herself more than anybody, Anna agreed.

~ ANNA ~

One day I got old. I looked in the glass of the travel agency and there was this grey-haired, grey-faced woman reflected – me, and not me. I counted back and couldn't find the last forty years. The poster of Vienna pulled me in. I still felt like that young Viennese woman, but when I looked sideways at my reflection, my nanna's image appeared. Like a time-traveller, I had taken on another body: colour drained, quickness spent, pleasure departed. Huge gaps in my life story erased the me who had once stood in Stephansplatz as the bells resounded on festival day. Everyone dressed in their dirndl and lederhosen flooded St. Stephan's cathedral for the special mass. Rays of light through the stained-glass windows poured through the smoke from the incense burners and over the worshippers; the faithful saintlike with their heads garlanded in clouds of colour. As the mass ended we shook back our lace scarves from our heads as if we were shaking off our sins, settled them on our shoulders and rose smiling. We lined up behind the men carrying Saint Stephan's banners chattering like the sparrows in the square outside, making our slow way out of the smoky rainbow towards the carved entrance. The men pushed the ponderous weight of the doors till they swung out and sunlight streamed in. They dipped the banners and we emerged into the bright light of the new day. In my nostrils, the clean smell of rain-washed trees, the rich perfume of the coffee, and the sugary scent of apple strudel. On my tongue, the thick coffee and the heavy, sweet cream of the pastry. In my ears, the gossip and the flirting.

'All gone,' she said, 'all gone.'

'Oh no,' Elizabeth put her coffee on the table and reached out to Anna. 'No, they still do it. We were there. John and I saw it.' Elizabeth remembered being hemmed in behind the crowd in the cathedral. Caught up in the excitement and the singing and the redolence of the incense. Enthralled by the long history of faithfulness.

Anna half smiled. 'I meant my friends.' Elizabeth swallowed heavily, and this time Anna reached out to her. 'But I'm glad it still happens.'

'Sorry,' she said and took Anna's outstretched hand, 'would you like to tell me about them?'

The following pension day the pair were outside the window again.

'I'm calling the police.' Katy was having a bad day; one airline had cancelled three flights causing her to reschedule several people booked on cruises and tours and more were threatening to do the same. 'They're stalking us.'

'They're just looking in the window, they're not doing anybody any harm,' Peter said, keeping his head down.

'You don't know what they've hidden in their shopping bags.'

'You think they're shoplifters?'

'I'm talking about weapons.' Katy's eyes narrowed.

'I can see a new soup ladle and a baguette hanging out of that one.' Peter peered through the window. 'Seems dangerous. We'd better call the food police.'

~ ELIZABETH ~

I guess you must use chicken if it is going to be called chicken soup. Well, if not, chicken stock maybe – and we can say the chicken walked through it – or maybe had a bath in among those vegetables – or peed it in. Carrots; soup always needs carrots, and onions – or maybe leeks – they taste good in soup. Sweeter and not as dominating. And then you just empty your vegetable drawer of all the bits and pieces. Everything tastes good with chicken – even if the bird only flew over the top of the pot. It's supposed to be very good for you – prophylactic the doctor said – but I guess you need to have some real chicken in there for it to do you any good. So, if you have the flu, real chicken soup is for you.

Sometimes I make mine with noodles and corn. A bit like Chinese soup – a real meal it is – fills you up. Better than those tins or packets. I could live on the stuff.

Have you tried it with parsley? I've got some in the garden. Growing a treat, it is, and just keeps coming up from seed all the time. Chop it over the top just before you serve it.

The soup bubbles away in the big red pot John bought for me, a gleam of fat on the top telling us that indeed a bird was sacrificed for our needs. Its fragrance permeates the house, filling the small cold corners and welcoming newcomers as the front door swings open and Molly barks her welcome.

I always loved the house being full of various smells – good ones of course – not blocked toilets or burnt potatoes. Who would have thought you could smell oranges all over the house or lemons when you squeezed them for lemon butter? Summer smells, all the fruits, particularly mangoes and peaches that come at Christmas and fill the whole house with their sweet ripeness. But chicken soup must be the best winter smell of all – and if you combine it with fresh cooked bread – enchanting.

John loved roast lamb best. Slow cooked so that its aroma grabbed you as you walked in through the front door and manhandled you all the way into the dining room. I was in the habit of putting it, frozen solid, into a slow oven and going off to church for the morning. We would worship together, have morning tea with our friends and do all the business we needed to and then return home to be ushered in by the fragrance of roasted meat. I'd put some veggies on and he'd open a bottle of wine while I made the mint sauce from our garden. After lunch we'd have a nap together – and maybe make love. A great way to start the week.

It seems like things will last forever. Chicken soup, slow cooked lamb, fresh summer oranges, lemon butter from our lemons, sweet love in the afternoon. They'll go on and on for others – but not for John and me.

So now I cook myself chicken soup.

'I've never cooked for one before.' Elizabeth was watching her reflection between the poster for a gourmet river cruise and one for hiking in New Zealand. 'I was married at nineteen, straight from home. John and I only had a year and then we had the children. Now there's just me and my dog, Molly. Sometimes I cook extra veggies for her, for old times' sake.'

She and Anna had been discussing Sacher Tort, wondering if the Coffee Pot would have some. Two reflections turned into three as a small Asian woman stood beside Anna.

'I miss it.' It was a small voice, but Anna and Elizabeth nodded in agreement without really defining that 'it' meant the same to all of them.

Elizabeth felt all her motherly instincts surge up into her bosom. 'I'm Elizabeth, this is Anna. Come and have coffee with us.'

~ KIM ~

I used to dream of having all my spices and sauces right next to my stove, so I could grab whatever I wanted as I cooked. My kitchen was so crowded and not enough cupboards. What I really wanted was to search and sniff out the right spice – a pinch of all-spice, or a shake of coriander or just a little fenugreek – so that the scent of my cooking would sneak like a ghost through the house, hunting my family till they came to ask what was for dinner. Now the family cooks for me. I visited my son's house and right next to the stove he has a cupboard full of herbs and spices. He stands at the stove and reaches out to the right for anything he needs. I don't mean to be envious, but he is so lucky. Simple pleasures, I say to him, as he cooks, and he understands.

'You'll have to share your recipes with us,' Elizabeth stated, 'we love food,' and looked at Anna for agreement.

Anna was nodding from habit. She remembered a time when she had enjoyed food, but lately everything tasted the same. She was trying to recall her favourite food when suddenly the long-forgotten scent of fresh strawberries popped into her head. 'I think I'll have a strawberry tart with my coffee,' she told the waitress.

Elizabeth looked up and smiled. 'What a good idea, I'll have some pecan tart.'

Kim, who had been going to order plain black coffee, suddenly laughed and said, 'I'll have a hot chocolate – on full cream milk.'

And they giggled away like a coven of school girls.

CHAPTER TWO

On the warm spring day that the women stood six abreast across his shop front, Peter decided to act.

Katy was threatening to leave. 'They're blocking the view.'

'Which view? Iceland, Ireland or Italy?' Peter doubted humour would help but it was worth a try – he couldn't face training another office assistant.

Katy gave him the death stare. For a while now, he'd thought that she'd been placing posters in the window to advertise her charms rather than seduce clients to travel. She seemed to enjoy watching the young yobos watching her through the window rather than at it. He couldn't blame them really. She was quite attractive if you liked pink hair, piercings, and black makeup. It was probably the short skirts under the open desk that clinched the attraction. Old ladies had seen it all before.

Time to do something about it then. He eyed the line-up. They looked like a broken denture – the original lady hunched and grey, her curly haired big friend, a tiny Asian lady, a tall willowy blonde hippie, a stately well-dressed woman, and one that that had a Cruella-de-Ville white streak through her otherwise dark-hair. Better watch that one, he thought. On second thoughts, he'd better watch all of them.

He rose from his computer, opened the front door, and popped his head out. He took a deep breath, ready to speak, and was nearly flattened by the combination of lavender and garlic – and he was sure he could sense a note of alcohol underneath the general old-lady smell. Regaining control, he addressed the throng: 'Can I help you, ladies?'

Six pairs of eyes swivelled toward him. Speaking eyes – filled with pleasure, surprise, annoyance, and guilt, all battling to gain the upper hand, so to speak, as they fought for words. They reminded him of a flock of doves, nodding, shuffling, a nearly universal denial until the last voice. 'Oh … no… no… no… well… yes please.' All heads turned back to that surprising 'yes.'

'Yes?' the chorus echoed.

'Yes?' Peter joined in.

Wide eyes were back on him again. He could feel the prickle of heat rising up his neck.

'Yes.' The large curly-haired woman spoke up, 'Do you have any old travel catalogues?' The doves bobbed their heads in unison. 'We don't mind what they are as long as they have lots of photos.'

'We like the pictures,' the Asian lady with a large shopping bag spoke up, 'they help us remember.'

'I don't need reminders,' the hunched woman added, and he realised she was the lone gazer who had started this show. Did he detect a middle European accent? 'I remember like it was yesterday,' she said and nodded at the poster of Vienna.

The heat had reached Peter's earlobes and he felt intoxicated by thoughts of other worlds. Katy coughed meaningfully behind him and he snapped back to the job at hand. What was he thinking to be caught up with these exotic suggestions? 'I'll… I'll see what I can find.' He retreated through the door and it shushed shut behind him.

'What do they want?' Katy glared through the glass.

'Brochures.'

'Brochures? What sort of brochures?'

'Old ones.'

'Old ones?'

'Old ones.' He felt the heat rising towards his scalp.

'If we give them some, will they go away?'

He hadn't thought to ask that question. He rather liked a window full of customers, even if they couldn't afford any holidays. 'There's a box of them somewhere.' Heading out the back, he grabbed the container and shot back through the front door before Katy could hammer him any further.

The women clustered around him like feeding time in the park and their hands started clawing in the box. 'Stand back.' The yes-woman was alpha bird: 'We'll take the lot.'

'All of them?' he gasped.

She nodded, 'Think of it as recycling.' She emptied the box into her gaping shopping trolley. 'Let's go. This will keep us going for ages.' And off they all waddled, trolley wheels tweeting, heading through the mall for the Coffee Pot two doors down.

The group had grown by word of mouth – the best advertising, they could have told their travel agency friends. Retired business-woman Di was neighbours with Patsy the hippy, as she had privately named her, and they had been meeting in the coffee shop long before the Travel Club started. They were swept up into the larger group like meteors vacuumed into a black hole. Kathryn had come along as a friend of Elizabeth's. She was stately, quiet and a good listener and often sat back just soaking up the exotic tales.

Kim had been sharing stories about her Vietnam, the country that they all remembered before the war that had ripped it apart. They were caught up in her family, her village and her nostalgia. Some also remembered friends and brothers who had gone to fight there.

'If I hadn't come here, I would never have met all of you,' said Kim. The women nodded over their tea and coffee and hot chocolate: 'It's like you have taken me to another world.'

'As you have taken us, Kim.' Patsy's soft words were singing their heart-songs.

'I thought I had forgotten my home, but here all the details come back. Do you know, when I dream I'm lost, I'm always looking for the house where I grew up? You would think after so many years living in Australia it would be my Australian home. But no. It is always my parents' home in the village where I was born. And I can feel the rough path beneath the soft soles of my sandals and smell the garlic and spices of dinner nearly ready and see those faces of the people so long lost that I loved so much.'

For once the only sound in the café was the hiss of the coffee machine as each of the women trod their own memory paths, looking for treasured faces, flashes of feelings, the scent of love. The lacy web of time called them along its strands, made more achingly beautiful by the gaps in their memories.

Peter grew used to the women at his window, and the yes-woman smiling benignly at him, and Katy as she came through to pick up the recycling. Parting with the old brochures caused the women to rapidly abandon the space in front of the shop, so Katy was happy to surrender the goods and regain her view.

'What do you think they do with them?' Katy, now intrigued, asked him one day.

'Recycle them?'

'Well hopefully – but what else first?'

He sighed and turned to her, 'They said it helped them remember.'

'Do they have old timers?'

'I don't know. Maybe.' He was rubbing his face with his hands. 'Or maybe they just want to remember their travels.' He turned back to the screen.

Katy leapt to her feet. 'Would you like a coffee?'

Peter felt his hands jump off the computer keyboard like frogs in a pond. It had been made abundantly clear to him that Katy was not there to fetch and carry for him. He was nothing if not well-trained.

'Cappuccino, please.' Seize the day, he thought, it may never come again, and he settled back into the computer space.

'Right.' Her hands were on her hips. 'I'm off to see what the Six Sisters are up to.'

He hid his smile. Katy had been trying out various names, like they were a rock group, and obviously come up with one that pleased.

She grabbed the petty cash purse and stomped off out the swinging door and down the mall.

At that morning hour the Coffee Pot had a serenity that lay over the vinyl-clad lounges like raincloud in a valley. The group in the back corner were oblivious to this – as they were to anybody enjoying the peace. They had pushed four tables together in a block and spread every surface with the glossy pictures of exotic destinations. The Asian lady had one in her hand and was hushing everybody as she began to speak in her quiet voice. Katy leaned toward the tables and heard, 'Fellow travellers,' then the rest was drowned out by the hiss of the coffee machine.

As the machine finished she heard one of the others cry out, 'I want that one.'

'No, tell us about that one,' said another woman.

And the Asian woman was speaking again in her low, musical voice.

Katy marched back into the office.

'Right. That's it. I've had it.'

Peter looked up. He could smell the cappuccino and, by the puffing and hissing, Katy looked like she had steamed up the milk for it herself. All that black make-up and she had become a dragon breathing fire.

'They're starting their own travel agency. AND they're using our brochures.'

'They're old brochures.' Peter looked back at his screen.

Katy was having none of this. 'They could book it online.'

'Did anybody have a smart phone?'

There was a head shake from Katy.

'Or a tablet?'

Again, the head shake.

'I know, a laptop. It was probably in the trolley.'

This time her head shook so hard her piercings rattled. 'You have to go and tell them they need to give the brochures back.'

Peter put his head down again and tried to look busy.

'Otherwise we'll lose business and then we'll have to close.'

He glued his eyes to the computer screen.

'And I'll take that job they offered me at Travel World.'

His stomach rolled over three times and his feet shot under him like an automaton. He found himself crossing the room, throwing open the door and, before he could say 'I don't care if you leave,' standing next to the table of women as though they had beamed him up to them.

'Oh look,' exclaimed the yes-woman, 'it's the nice young man from the travel agency. Would you like to join us?'

Why, he thought, are you coming apart? He certainly was.

'Would you like a cappuccino?' the yes-woman asked, and he was trying to remember how he came to be seated around the table with them. 'It's the least we can do for our benefactor.' They all giggled.

Wow, he thought, two free coffees in one morning, entirely forgetting that the first one was still at the shop, hot and ready and bought with his own petty cash. He was trying to think of a polite way of asking what the hell they were up to when the Asian lady reached out and took his hand.

'Thank you so much for these. They have changed our lives.'

And then it hit him. He remembered the long, lined, sad faces through the shop window. Now their smiles glowed with an inner fire.

'We've been travelling,' The middle-European woman looked

around at the others for assurance. They dutifully nodded. 'All over the world.'

'Would you like to come with us?' chimed in the hippie.

By the time Peter walked back through the glass doors, his first cappuccino was cold and his assistant was boiling. He gave her a crocodile smile. She had expected repentance but there was none of that in his unhinged attitude.

'They're just talking,' he said.

One of her eyebrows rose.

'Reminiscing,' he added.

Her other eyebrow joined the scepticism.

'Telling each other their travel stories.'

Her lips pursed but the eyebrows slowly descended like two pigeons coming to roost.

What he didn't tell her was that he had enjoyed every nanosecond of it. Travelling with the senior ladies was invigorating. Hardened by the years of organising good times for others, his heart and mind had found a way back to why he loved travel in the first place. In fact, he hadn't felt so buoyant since he was a boy.

'Next time *you* can go with them.'

The piercings in her eyebrows shot up like clay pigeons.

Boom, he thought. Gotcha.

~ PATSY ~

'You see that old man in the bed over there.'

The nurse glanced across the room to where the elderly woman was pointing and saw the supine, desiccated figure propped part way up to enable his laboured breathing. She nodded.

'I don't... I mean, I don't see an old man. I see my husband, my darling, my lover. The man who has been my intimate companion for over sixty years. We met when he was seventeen and I was not quite sixteen and he taught me everything I

know about intimacy – and I'm not just talking about the sexual kind. Although that has been good enough and kept on right up until when he ended in that bed.'

Too much information the nurse was thinking.

'He smiles at me and I see the eager boy in his best outfit I fell in love with. I see him walking through the front door after work. I remember his excitement when he retired, and we went travelling, finding new places, exotic cities and strange people to talk to. A turn of the head and I see him with his mother – and mine for that matter – as we cared for them together when they reached the end of their lives. He opens his eyes and looks across the room and I remember how he commanded the respect and love of all who knew him.'

The nurse smiled stiffly.

'I see him working with me in our garden. Nothing better than a day spent outside together and then a swim and a glass of wine and falling on each other. When he moans I remember how my touch brought his arousal and how we would lay naked, locked in each other's arms afterwards. And how he would sleep a little then caress me and we would talk about all sorts of secrets. We did our best garden plans at those times.'

Tears welled in the nurse's eyes.

'So, when I said I would like to get into bed with him, it wasn't a request, I mean to do it.'

The nurse raised her eyebrows, nodded and, moving across the room, let down the side of the bed and gently shifted the old man a little towards her. He roused slightly and opened his eyes. Patsy took off her shoes, put them neatly under his bed, took down the other bed side and climbed into the narrow, empty space, resting her head on his chest. Opening his eyes slightly, he looked down at the grey head and put his hand on it. 'My girl,' he said in a voice like ancient paper sliding sideways and they both shut their eyes.

'At least they're not naked,' muttered the nurse. 'Well, not yet anyway.'

'It was so romantic floating down the Nile in one another's arms.' Patsy was far away, looking out across the mall, but seeing instead the green, reedy banks and the dark-skinned boys on their fragile rafts poling their way along through river sedges – and the donkeys walking around and around, drawing water from the Nile, as they had for a millennia, to water the narrow rim of green before the desert.

'We pretended we were in *Death on the Nile* – decadent, upper-class snobs knocking off their enemies. How we laughed.'

The women all took a deep breath and talked at once. 'Did you see the Valley of the Kings? ... Did you visit the Cairo Museum? ... Did you climb the pyramids? Did you ride a camel?' Patsy laughed at the last one.

As Katy approached the table of bubbling women, Patsy was facing her. 'Oh look!' An assortment of white, grey and dyed heads swivelled towards her like the clown game at the Easter show: 'It's that beautiful girl from the travel agent.' Patsy extended a beckoning hand towards Katy. 'I love all your rings – so exotic – they remind me of Egypt. I always think of you as Cleopatra.'

And wham, bam, thank you, mam – the women had a new best friend.

Katy didn't tell Peter what the women had said about her. She didn't tell him that she was going to buy that jewelled kaftan from the shop next door to the Coffee Pot or that the new add to her wish list was to travel to Egypt to visit Alexandria, where Cleopatra had reigned. The idea was still humming in her head, making her glide through the shop, filling her mind with new make-up possibilities.

'They're quite nice, you know – cute really.' Katy flashed him a cool smile.

'Who?' Peter played along.

'The Six Sisters.'

'Oh, you mean the Travel Club.'

'Is that what they are?'

'That's what they call themselves. Did they talk about travel while you were there?'

Katy stood with one foot pressed on top of the other, considering her answer. 'Not exactly… but … I guess … sort of.' When she tried to remember the conversation, it slipped away and all that came to mind was the warmth of the women towards each other – and to her. While they shared their journeys in travel, in love, in life, she had been trying to remember the last time she had been included in a convocation of women. Almost a foreign country, she had thought, as exotic to her as she was to them. But the sweetness, the sheer inclusiveness of the experience, poured over her like honey and stuck to her soul. It would take hours to answer Peter's question – if she could ever find an answer – if she could expose the glow in her gut that had nothing and everything to do with the hot chocolate they had bought her – when she could come to terms with the fact that the feeling was welling up way past the short half hour she had spent at the Coffee Pot. 'I'll tell you later,' she said, knowing that she would not.

~ DI ~

Since I left work, I feel slower. Like I stopped and enjoyed the stopping and don't want to start again. Or don't know how to start again on my own. I remember as a child, before TV and computers, we shared our lives. Families and friends made occasions to talk. Birthday parties, card parties, dinner parties, over the fence with neighbours, watering the garden together on hot summer nights swatting mossies off bare legs. People went to bed at the same time rather than binging on TV. I remember apparently endless years, talking and talking with my sister as we lay in our beds until Mum would bellow at us 'Go to sleep'. *Nights are so quiet on my own. And silent days stretch long. But since I've been having coffee with the Travel Club, my voice is coming back.*

Now, I want to write – not the official blurb as was required by my job – but interesting narratives. Maybe be an author. But I need authority, confidence, a voice, a history, a her-story, or perhaps many voices and stories. The problem is I no longer know who or what I am. I needn't hurry. I won't be missed. I have become no-one. This is how we fade into the end of our lives – gradually handing over responsibilities, altering our days, sloughing off the old self to find an unencumbered person beneath – unrecognisable to ourselves and others alike.

It's not threat of death that scares us – it's the impenetrable beauty of life that's terrifying – and the thought that every day should be precious but bowls over us like a rolling pin – until our days are flat and infertile. It happened again as I cleaned out the old cupboard – that paralysing regret, so I could hardly throw things out – as if I'd skipped too quickly over the bounty of living and somehow thrown my life away. That's what I'd like to capture.

'Here's a place I've never been – Iran.' Di held up the brand-new brochure.

Peter gulped the hot coffee, choked, and Elizabeth thumped him on the back. He had seen the pamphlet come in and thrown it into the recycling box because he doubted the safety of visiting such a place. 'Hmm,' he said 'Iran.' He also doubted whether he wanted to organise anybody to go there, travel insurance being what it was.

'What a history! Do you know there's ten thousand years of history there?' Di was getting excited. Peter thought privately that most history revolved around people killing other people. But Di was not to be stopped. 'I'd like to go there and see it. I have a lovely Iranian neighbor who has been telling me all about the historic sites. I'd love to write about them and capture it all on film.'

'Would she go back with you and show you?' Peter asked.

Di looked a bit miffed. 'Of course not, it's not safe for her there.'

'Why?'

'She was a feminine activist when she was younger and came out with her family to be safe.'

'Why don't you write her story?' Elizabeth suggested.

Di's mouth and eyes simultaneously opened wide. She collected herself. 'Maybe I will.'

'So,' murmured Anna, her gaze fixed on Peter, and then her voice a little stronger, 'what's your story?'

Peter's head moved from side to side of its own volition, 'I don't have a story.'

'Everybody has a story,' said Anna, patting him on the arm, 'one day you'll tell us yours.'

'For now, tell us about how to travel in the Middle East,' Di said in a determined voice. Although, privately, she was promising to go home and capture her neighbor's story.

It was Katy who noticed that the Six Sisters had become five. The quiet one, with her carefully coiffed hair and cropped nails, had been missing for a couple of weeks now. Peter never counted them. To him they were a wall of women across the shopfront and, if that wall was a little less wide, he thought himself lucky.

'I wonder where she's gone.' Katy said slowly.

'Gone. Who's gone?'

'The Queen Mother.'

Peter took a moment to process the fact that Katy actually knew who the Queen Mother was. He looked Katy full in the face and let out an astonished laugh.

'What?' she said, 'You don't think I know about the Queen Mother. She's the Queen's mother – der – well she was. I'll have you know my nanna always wanted to be like the QM. She said they had a lot in common – both loving jigsaws and all that.'

'Which one's the QM then?' he turned away to hide his smile.

'The quiet, queenly one. You know – gets her hair done every week, always made up, dressed up, stockings and skirts and never any frills.' She didn't say the one whose smile made her remember sitting on Nanna's knee, snuggled up against her chenille dressing gown – or how black the world had looked when Nanna left it.

'My turn this week,' said Katy, 'see you in an hour.' And she was out of the shop with a whoosh of the door before Peter could object to the extended coffee break. At least it was quiet now, he thought, he could do some work. Though, perhaps, it was a bit too quiet.

~ KATHRYN ~

What a privilege it is to teach somebody who really wants to learn. To watch them grow their skills and knowledge as they happily do what you ask them to do. Wonderful to know, after 40 years of teaching, that it is of value and that nothing you ever teach is lost. Sometimes it's translated into other places or genres, but it remains as much a part of the person as their eye colour or the shape of their face. It's like you're weaving it gently and firmly into their genes. Then you enjoy their return with their own children – passing on the knowledge you engendered in them – like one unending family. And then they move on and leave you behind.

Kathryn patted her carefully coiffed hair into place as she took her seat. 'I'm thinking of giving up music teaching.' She stared into her swirling tea as she stirred it.

'Why would you do that?' Elizabeth asked.

Kathryn shrugged one shoulder. She didn't really know why. It was a feeling that had been mushrooming inside her since the last lot of exams. It was the impatience she felt with students' behaviour that she'd once accepted. All that work and effort and worry she put into each of them – then the ones that really cared and worked hard lost it on the day while others sailed through.

'It's such a struggle to get kids to practise these days. All that technology – games and videos – it's as if doing something real is beyond them.'

Elizabeth well remembered the challenge of getting her boys to practice when Kathryn taught them. 'I wonder whether it's also parents not encouraging practice.'

'Maybe,' Kathryn sipped her Earl Grey tea, 'there's certainly a lot more of that around. The problem is you must practise to succeed –

and then success pushes you to grow more. And somehow, I've lost the will to push. It's as though I've forgotten why I first loved music and now I'm lost in this discord.'

Katy was sitting quietly, lulled by the ebb and flow of the women's words, thinking how much she would have loved to learn the piano. No money for that in her childhood.

'I learned music as a child in Austria.' Anna spoke quietly. 'After the war they were trying to restart the Music Conservatory. I had no piano to practise on, but a neighbour let me play hers. It reminded her of her son who was killed on the Eastern Front.'

Anna seemed so tired and time-worn it was difficult to think of her as a child. All the things we don't know about each other, thought Elizabeth, could fill an ocean.

'Do you still play?' Kathryn smiled at Anna.

'I don't know. It's been so long. Perhaps I would remember if I tried. Perhaps not.'

'Are you feeling okay?' Elizabeth asked Kathryn who had missed their meeting place at the travel agency and had wandered into the Coffee Pot later.

'I'm just tired. I think I need a holiday.'

'Well,' said Katy, hearing the magic word, 'You've come to the right place.' They all laughed. 'Where are we going today?'

'Anywhere,' Kathryn replied, then added sotto voce, 'but here.'

As she left the café, Katy noticed Kathryn giving Anna a card. 'Come around some time and play my piano,' she was saying. Anna was shaking her head. 'I insist,' declared Kathryn in a firm QM voice, 'let's see what you remember. And perhaps you can show me some of the things you were taught in Vienna.'

The following Thursday, Peter came through the door with a cappuccino and a hot chocolate.

'This is nice,' said Katy. She was thinking it was a bit spooky, he'd never done this before.

'Make the most of it, they close tomorrow.'

'Who?'

'The Coffee Pot. Can't afford the rent they say, now that new food court's opening upstairs.'

'So, can we?' Katy asked.

'Afford the rent?' Peter seemed confused at her concern. Katy nodded at him. 'At present we can – just. But we need to pick up our sales a bit.' He sounded a bit anxious about the rising rent.

'What will the Six Sisters do?'

'I guess they'll move to the food court upstairs.' He hadn't given his recyclers a second thought.

'But the tables will be screwed down. How will they spread out all their brochures?'

'I don't know.' If he wasn't screwed, he thought. The figures he had worked on last night were running through his head – and the thought that the partners in his business would expect a full report soon. You would think your brother and sister would be understanding, but he had found it was not necessarily so.

'I know – we could set up a table and chairs for them here.' Peter's attention snapped back to see Katy waving her arms around like a windmill as she spoke. At first, he thought he had misheard her. No – she wouldn't say that. Surely not. Here? In his tidy, quiet, organised shop? This was a business. 'We could buy a coffee machine and get cookies and make a conversation corner.' His head was shaking back and forth. He wanted to say *call them biscuits not cookies* – and *we're not a charity* – or even a good solid *NO* – but nothing was coming out his mouth. 'Like – it's only once a fortnight on pension day. They'll be no trouble. I'll look after them.'

And now his head was nodding up and down, up and down, like the velvet dog in the back of his mother's car.

CHAPTER THREE

The first time they met in the Travel Agency it was bedlam. Well, that's what Peter told Katie later.

'What's Bedlam?'

'Bedlam used to be the place they sent crazy people.'

'They're not crazy.' Katy sniffed, and Peter couldn't tell whether it was allergy or outrage.

'No. We are. What possessed me to agree to having them here?'

'You know you like them.' She nudged him with her elbow, and he sidled away like a startled cat. 'And did you see people stopping and looking in the shop while they were here? One man actually came in and stood for ages staring at the brochure wall pretending to look but he was listening to them.' She nodded towards conversation corner as if the women were still there.

Peter had noticed the people looking through the window – not the usual yobbos – but Katy didn't seem to mind. And yes, a couple had come in and sat for some time asking him questions and Katy had offered them coffee as well. It was all very chummy. If they decided to book with him he might change his mind – well maybe not yet but he could at least consider updating his opinion.

Of course, now they were meeting in the shop both he and Katy were involved in the conversation.

'Did you see the QM chatting with the European lady?' Katy just had to comment.

'They were all talking at once,' Peter growled.

'I meant at the end – when everybody left – they walked away together – and they were like – really close.'

Peter had been too busy cleaning up. 'All those crumbs,' he muttered.

'Would you like to come and have some lunch with me?' Kathryn asked Anna. She had tried Elizabeth's recipe and she noticed the fresh bread in Anna's bag. 'The chicken soup is in the slow cooker and we could try out some more of those Diabelli duets.'

Despite the coffee and biscuits, Anna's stomach rumbled at the thought of soup. She nodded and settled into a slow pace beside her friend. As they passed through the automatic doors to the main street the autumn wind blew through her thin cardigan. She buttoned it up more tightly over her vanished waistline and reminded herself that Viennese autumns were icy compared to this. Must be getting soft, she mused, and then was caught up in what Kathryn was saying.

'I had this new student last week. Honestly, I don't know what they teach them these days. Can't read rhythm to save her life and the notes in the bass clef are a mystery to her. She can play simple pieces but her last teacher would just say *put your hands here and copy me*.'

Anna shook her head. She remembered how, in that far-off time, her teachers had made her count rhythm and walk around clapping rhythm against the beat of her feet, until it invaded her soul and her whole body reverberated with it. Did nobody care about good learning any more – well Kathryn did. The wonderful thing was that, with her friend's help, all the knowledge she had thought lost was gradually making its way to the surface. Like long-dead voices it slipped through slowly at first, note by note, and then suddenly broke out of her fingers on the keys in an orgasmic explosion. It was almost as if it was playing her: it had lain dormant all those years, waiting for the power source to be regained so it could burn, and bubble and burst forth with great joy. Her visits to Kathryn's had been purely musical up until now – an exchange of knowledge. She bartered the chance to participate in music for her history, her birthright, her stories of old Europe which she for so long thought valueless in this place. Hardly fair, she thought, she was getting by far the best of the exchange.

'I would love to come for lunch,' she said shyly, 'but only if you will agree to come to my unit and let me prepare you a Viennese meal next time.'

The morning Peter brought a whole apple strudel in for pension day Katy knew she had won the war.

There had been brief skirmishes around the office regarding the cost of the morning tea, the space that they took up, and the general riotousness of the women's conversation. Katy enthusiastically defended the women but had been at a loss to predict whether they would end up on the winning side. What she had noticed, and obviously Peter had as well, was that their exuberance and storytelling was attracting other customers – and those customers were coming back and booking.

The deciding battle had occurred when the Asian lady, who she now knew as Kim, had broken out of her conversation with the other women to come over and tell a couple of potential customers about the beauties of Vietnam. Katy had gone to get the husband and wife some tea and, by the time she returned with it, the three were deep in conversation.

On the way out, she passed Peter's desk and was struck by the look of desperate horror on his face. It occurred to her it was because she had actually left clients in the hands of one of the Six Sisters. Katy stifled the laughter rising from her belly and made it all the way to the urn before she started shaking with glee. Five minutes later, her control restored, she returned with the tea and noticed that Peter's face now wore a look of stunned bemusement – like a garden ornament, she thought – as he watched the clients warm to the conversation and ask questions from the brochures.

'It was always such a busy place – full of bicycles, you know,' Kim was telling them, 'but beautiful. They called it the food bowl, you know, because fruit and vegetables grew all year round.'

'When did you come to Australia?'

'In 1980. My husband had fought with the army in the south, so we were treated very badly by the communists. It took a long time to save money to pay and the first time the man who promised the boat took our money and then there was no boat, so we had to save again. It was difficult. If the communists found you had been putting money away, they would send you away to a retraining camp. What would our children do then?' Kim was tiptoeing those laneways again. She could feel the warm scented air and see her home.

The husband of the couple was nodding at her. 'I have a friend who's a Vietnam Vet. He told me it was very bad after Saigon fell.' Katy felt her heartbeat quicken. What was Kim going to say next? Her stomach tightened at the thought that that this was bringing up old sadness for Kim, worried that the couple would be put off their holiday, and worse still she knew Peter was eavesdropping. She glanced back over her shoulder at him. He had his head down and seemed to be hyperventilating.

When she looked back, Kim was wavering. 'Yes, it was terrible,' Kim took a deep breath, shut her eyes and then blessed them with a warming smile, 'but now my children have been back, and they say it is beautiful again. So much history. Ancient and modern. And you can cruise the Mekong now too.' This was sounding better, thought Katy. 'Perhaps you will visit my village.' Katy wasn't sure about this new suggestion, but Kim was writing it in English and Vietnamese on a piece of paper and handing it to the couple: 'Please take some pictures if you do and…' Kim stopped as she tried to work out how she could see those photos.

As she sat down again, Katy said, 'You can email them here. I'll share them with Kim.' The couple nodded happily, and the elderly Vietnamese lady hugged Katy.

'You are such a good girl.' Kim whispered into her shoulder, and the hot-chocolate feeling bubbled up in Katy's insides, washed through her veins and poured warmth from her head to her toes.

'Did you put her up to it?' Peter asked as they were locking up for the night.

Katy simply shook her head. She thought about pretending she didn't know what he was talking about just to wind him up, but it seemed to trivialise the wonder of Kim's words.

'They booked the holiday?'

Katy nodded. 'On the spot.'

'Wow,' whispered Peter.

'Yes, wow. And before they go they want to meet with Kim again for more information on places to see. Then the husband talked about introducing his Vietnam Vet friend to Kim's whole family.'

'Wow.' He was on repeat. Vaccinated with a gramophone needle, Nanna would have said. Finally, she had surprised him. Well, it was not really her surprise, more the Six Sisters' effect.

'Do you think we could do this more often?' she asked.

He shrugged. 'How would you pull it off?' He locked the door behind them.

'Not sure. Let's think about it.'

'Katy.' She turned in her stride and looked back to him. He was smiling. 'Why don't we ask them?'

She found herself nodding, smiling back, chest aching with joy. And she headed off into a brave new world of marketing possibilities.

The next pension day, Peter arrived with the apple strudel.

~ PETER ~

I seem to have spent all my days wishing my life away. Wishing to be older – got my wish there. Wishing winter was summer and the heat of summer would wash away into winter – wishing I was on holidays – or maybe just far away from here. Wishing mum was somebody else's responsibility – still feel guilty about that wish. Wishing, wishing, wishing, and now I wish I could have some of those moments back again – the good ones, of course. I wish I could be twenty again and know what I know now.

Uncle Felix used to say he wished he could be young again and know what he knew then. He died at 48. Although the Vietnam war taught him things I hope I never learn. Funny the words you remember people saying so far away. I must have been about twelve when he said that – or maybe it was his mantra – and I really had no idea what he was talking about. Life was very straight-forward at twelve. You went to school, watched TV, weekends were for sport and visiting, you tried to figure out what adults expected of you and kept your head down. And you read lots and lots of books about people who really lived. And you wished you were older, so you could live. Now I know what I know, it's the value of those everyday experiences that is so precious – I realise the worth of the mundane. All the characters in the books I read were reaching out towards a happy existence – which I had and didn't value. They all had problems and quests and unsolved mysteries that wrecked their lives. What they wanted was love and peace and stability – a happy life.

I guess we don't know what we have until we lose it. There is no one happy place, it comes from inside us.

'Well, ladies,' Peter had been thinking about how he could say this. Was proposition the right word? Proposal? Suggestion? No, that was a bit weak. They were all looking at him holding the whole apple strudel. 'Are you ready to be propositioned?' That was not what he had meant to say but it certainly lightened the mood. He noticed Elizabeth, the yes-woman blush, Kim look away, Anna laughing in her hand and the others looking – was that interest? He hoped not.

'Let's have some coffee and tea first and I'll tell you about our plan.' They cut up the apple strudel and poured the tea and coffee and sat down to talk about how they could help the agency. Kim's eyes fell in embarrassment when Peter praised her conversation with the couple, but the other women applauded her. 'I was just being friendly,' she whispered.

'That's why it was so beautiful,' Peter assured her, 'and sincere.' He gave them time to absorb this idea. He looked sideways at Katy and she was nodding enthusiastically, egging him on. 'We're wondering if you'd like to share your experiences with other customers. We get people interested in visiting places all over the world and, in this day of internet booking, we thought some wise words and the personal touch might increase our business.'

'You want us to help?' Elizabeth was wide eyed.

'Well, yes, but only if you want to,' said Peter. 'We can't really afford to pay you, but we thought you could talk to people and tell them about foreign places,' he took a deep breath, 'and we would give you as much morning and afternoon tea as you can eat.'

'And lunch, if it was lunch time,' put in Katy.

Anna looked Peter in the eye, 'We would help you anyway, you're our friends.' Peter heard Katy sigh behind him. 'But if you feed us, all the better.' There was a gale of laughter around the table.

'Tell us what you want us to do.' Di was getting enthusiastic now. She could taste the excitement, not coffee or strudel or even chocolate cake but the burning steel of adrenalin.

Katy whipped six forms out of her desk drawer. 'Just write in these where you've been and when. If you've lived there or been there or even seen the place. In Australia as well as overseas.' They all nodded. 'And please write your names and contact numbers so we can keep in touch.'

Peter beamed over his cappuccino and apple strudel and felt a deep warmth that made his whole being relax back into the chair. The ball was in their court, as his mother would say.

CHAPTER FOUR

'I need to get to know them better,' Peter told Katy a week or so after the women had accepted his offer.

'Read the surveys,' she said through the side of her mouth, eyes firmly fixed on her screen.

'I have read them.'

She looked across and rolled her eyes at him, 'Read them again.' She inhaled deeply. 'Maybe make them into a list so you know what they have in common.'

A tiny bright bubble bloomed in Peter's brain with the caption *she is the secretary and I am the boss*. Could he share the thought with her? Hmmm, maybe not. And reading the surveys made him increasingly aware of the women as people. Of course, he saw them through the prism of their travel journeys and where they had lived, but the surveys also asked if they had travelled alone and revealed relationships. Katy had included where they were born and grew up, their marital status and their children and grandchildren. This had made him feel uncomfortable, so he had urged her to explain to the women that they did not have to answer all the questions if they would rather not.

'I'll take them home tonight and see what I can come up with,' he heard himself saying. Really, he thought, I should have something better to do after work. But a new caption appeared – *this beats hands down playing computer solitaire or watching reality TV*.

'I put together some figures,' he told Katy the next day. 'I've emailed them to you.'

'I saw,' replied Katy – not sure what to say next. She had already been working on how better to gather the information, so they could use it as a marketing tool. Peter had drawn up a list of statistics for the whole group, complete with pie charts and graphs. He was preening over his diagrams and Katy pursed her black lips as she thought how to put her opinion to him – gently.

'I like this.' She pointed to the list of countries with the names beside and the length of time each woman had spent there, 'and this.' This was a pie chart showing backgrounds of the women. 'Let me think about what else we could do. They are all so interesting.'

Peter smiled at her. 'Yes, they are.' He looked out the window at a vision of the Six Sisters only he could see. 'Wonderful, really.'

Katy's eyes opened wide and filled up. Her head was nodding without any control from her brain and she turned away to hide her flushing face.

Where possible, the women decided to meet weekly, instead of just on pension day, so Peter or Katy could brief them on upcoming appointments.

The first thing they did was to look at the two maps: one of the world, and one of Australia, with their names on all the places they had been. There were clusters in some places – certainly in Australia – but also around Europe. All the better, Peter mused, he could have more than one of the sisters at a time to talk to prospective travellers. Better be careful though, he didn't want to overwhelm either the women or his clients.

Katy had also suggested they install a big screen on the wall behind the Travel Club table where they could play travel shows or display people's photos. This was instigated by Kim's Vietnam travellers. They had been delighted to share the photos of their trip and the whole Travel Club supported Kim as she soaked up the images. Hanoi in the north was their first stop, a place Kim had never been. The markets and tree-lined streets were beautiful, and then on to Halong Bay with its rocky pillars like standing stones in the sea. Peter thought he would get out the posters he had of this place and put them around to entice people. It was certainly luring him to book a trip – he could almost taste the salt air and the spicy food. On then down the coast through picturesque fishing villages and the endless gaudy green of paddy fields and into Ho Chi Min City, once called Saigon. Kim's eyes were luminous with unshed tears. More fascinating photos of the floating markets in the Mekong Delta and finally the village where she was born. A special day trip at the end of their tour, the couple said. Kim stood and slowly walked over to the screen, her hand held high against its heat as if she could feel the texture of the buildings, the stony path beneath her feet and the faces of the townsfolk – strangers but eerily familiar.

'Thank you,' she whispered – and although her back was to them, each person felt the depth of her gratitude without knowing if it was meant for them.

'No,' said the wife of the couple, 'thank you.'

'A two tissue-box day,' Katy told Peter afterwards, as they sniffled together.

'I'm going to have these maps printed as posters and put them up on the wall,' announced Katy.

'Why?' Peter was not being difficult – well not very difficult – just curious.

'Because I want to.'

'And?'

'And I think people might be interested.'

'Clients? Why would they be interested?' Now she had him going.

'Well,' Katy was carefully considering her words, 'if we offer a personal experience to our clients, let's show them what's available in terms of destinations.' She stopped and looked around the walls covered in travel advertisements. 'What if I asked the women for an old photo of them when they were there,' she pointed at the maps, 'and take a good photo of each of them now and display it as *The Travel Club*.'

Peter scratched his head, so his curly fair hair stood on end. It was certainly different from any travel agency display he had ever seen. 'Let's ask the Sisters.' He smiled widely at Katy and added, 'Great creativity, well done.'

Wow, thought Katy, he looks really happy, and hot, and ten years younger… is he too old for me? She quickly dismissed the thought. Maybe the Six Sisters have somebody we could hook him up with. Just gotta make sure he smiles at her.

The women all agreed to their photos being up there, although there was chaos in the agency when the current pictures were taken. They were all primping and preening themselves and each other until Katy got them in hand.

'Everybody SIT down.' She spoke firmly in Nanna voice. They did it – what a surprise she thought. 'You all look wonderful. '

'Can you make us look younger?' asked Di.

'I don't want to.' Katy smiled shyly at her. 'I want people to know that you know your stuff. That we value your years of experience. That you can tell them things that travel companies don't know and if they do, won't say. You,' and she made great use of the dramatic pause she had also learned from Nanna, 'are our experts.'

After that it was easy. She took several pictures of each of the women and of the whole group – and then they insisted on one with her and one with Peter. Elizabeth then ducked into the dress shop next door and strong-armed one of the shop assistants into coming in and taking a photo of everybody.

They pored over the photos for ages. 'These digital cameras are wonderful,' said Kathryn.

'Wait till you see what I do with the pictures,' Katy winked at her, much to Kathryn's surprise, 'and the old ones you've brought to scan.'

By the following week, the whole display was up on the wall complete with photos and maps. Local shopkeepers kept calling in to see what all the fuss was about. The butcher, the baker, and the dressmaker – Katy had said to Peter, ignoring the hairdresser because they annoyed each other. The women were entranced. Peter a little less so. He had completely lost a huge area of the wall space. Oh well, he'd made other people happy, maybe he'd just be more selective about what went up. Or delegate to Katy – what a good idea.

Now the shop's regular visitors were the local shopkeepers. Their favourite question was whether the Travel Club offered discounts.

'No, no, it's not that sort of club,' said Peter, 'just memories, experiences, and food.'

The butcher down the way laughed. 'I do that every day,' he assured them, 'and discounts too.'

The garrulous hairdresser upstairs said she didn't do the food but offered the first two, plus counselling. 'You have to study psychology to be a hairdresser. You need to know what's in the head as well as what's on it.'

Three of the women were coming in to the agency as she said this and they all laughed. Kathryn visited the salon every week and Elizabeth only when she needed to. 'You give me a cup of coffee,' said Kathryn.

'That's because you're such a good customer,' the hairdresser told Kathryn, with a sly glance at Elizabeth who was spasmodic at best about her appearance and preferred the travel agency coffee.

Anna, Kathryn, and Elizabeth had an appointment to talk to some prospective clients who wanted to know about Vienna. Anna was to talk about the historical aspects of the city; Kathryn, the music; and

Elizabeth, a more modern view as a tourist. Peter was impressed at their preparation. Their talk was excellent. All three couples booked a cruise with him there and then, and went away electric with excitement about Vienna, and the other places along the river. That day the strudel slid down very easily.

~ KATY ~

I used to dream I was a Russian Princess. Wrapped in furs, I would slide across the ice on my silver skates. Draped in diamonds, I would glide across the marble floors of my palace. It was all Nanna's fault. 'Too many fairy stories,' Dad always said. 'Filling her head with nonsense and calling her "Princess".' He'd hardly look up from the footy as he grumbled. Nanna would wink at me and poke her tongue out at the back of his head. And we would shake with the laughter held tight in our bellies. Nanna was a rebel, but she loved all things Russian – well maybe not Stalin – or Rasputin – or vodka – she said gin was her tipple – Mother's Ruin she called it. I was sixteen when I decided vodka was okay and I gradually learned about Stalin and Rasputin and agreed with her that you wouldn't want to meet them on a dark night – or even in broad daylight.

I can't remember ever thinking of myself as ordinary until after she died. When she wasn't around anymore, I would lay at night imagining her in the places in her stories. Marching down Red Square, her solid figure dominating the revolution, or dancing half-naked in the winter palace, or the two of us under furs shushing through the snow in a lanterned troika. She always said shushing about snow – she'd never seen snow but could imagine it. In fact, she had never left Australia, or Sydney for that matter. Dad pointed that out to me at her funeral.

I often wondered if she was a time traveller because our journeys were so real. There wasn't a book about Russia in all the local libraries that we hadn't totally digested, and all around her room, interspersed with family photos, were pictures of Russia. The prize of the collection was a film poster from Doctor Zhivago *with Omar Sharif swathed in furs. She would sing me to sleep when I was small with* Lara's Theme *from the movie. 'Somewhere, my love,' she would croon, 'there will be songs to sing.' After she was gone I heard the end of the song and realised it was a farewell. I sang it quietly to Nanna as she lay in her casket. Dad turned his back on my grief. But I didn't let that stop me, I sang it right to the end. 'Farewell, my love, till we shall meet again.'*

Rebelliousness must be genetic because, the moment I realised I was quite ordinary, I started wearing the black lipstick and, somehow, I bought clothes that went with it. Every time I got a new piercing, I swore to her that one day I would have a diamond to put in it. Funny how you remember these things. For so long I was obsessed with memories of old Russia – well, really memories of Nanna's version of old Russia. It was the posters of the Kremlin that made me take a travel course. My friends said they would never have guessed that my virtual existence would end up creating reality for others. Or that I could live amongst those snowy snaps on the travel store window.

As winter rolled on, the women decided to expand their experiences and hear about places they had never seen.

'Iceland!' exclaimed Anna one cold, drizzly day, 'really! Iceland!' She gaped at Peter who had told them this was now the number one destination. 'When I lived in Europe, we thought going to Iceland was like being sent to Siberia. I knew some Danes whose parents worked for the government. They were sent there before the war for a couple years. Couldn't wait to come back to Copenhagen.' She motioned towards the shoppers outside the window with their thick jumpers and dripping umbrellas. 'This is summer in Iceland.' Everybody laughed.

Peter realised he was enjoying himself. Each week he was finding places they'd never seen. Katy's survey had given him the details of their lives and the women had enjoyed endless conversations about what they knew of where they'd been that had whetted his appetite to travel again. There was a hunger in his gut and he wasn't sure what to do about it.

Katy came over with a plate of cupcakes and offered them around.

'Where's Kathryn?' she asked the group.

'Sick,' said Elizabeth, looking at the bright pink cupcake in her hand, 'can we take her one of these?' Katy nodded and went to find something to wrap it in.

'Who would have ever thought little cakes could be such big business?' Elizabeth was shaking her grey curly head like a poodle. 'I used to make them all the time with my children. We'd end up with batter everywhere. You know, you'd show them how to dollop it into the patty cake papers and it would stick to the paper and lift it out of the pan as they raised the spoon and then it would be all over everybody.'

Peter wondered had his mother done that with him? He thought he remembered little cakes as a child and considered all the precious moments you lose when someone's gone.

The other women were smiling, lost in the memories of other children, or in regret they had never had the chance to try this, or in smugness that their kitchens were always clean and tidy.

Katy remembered making cakes with her nanna who never used a cookbook and cooked by smell – *when it smells cooked, it is cooked was her motto. 2,4,6,8 is the only recipe you need to remember* Nanna would say – and Katy did remember it – 2 eggs, 4 oz butter, 6 oz sugar, 8 oz of flour and half a cup of milk, or orange juice, or something wet. Just needed to convert the ounces to grams. Nanna had been bilingual in measurements. And anyway, 6oz of sugar was one cup and 8oz of flour was two. She was drifting off. Would her father appreciate it if she made a cake tonight? Probably – he liked sweet things – and he'd been a bit fluey this week, it might cheer him up. Or else it would make him think she was a bit odd again. That's good, she decided, keep him guessing.

'Has Kathryn got the flu?' she asked Anna.

'Just a heavy cold, she says.' Anna pursed her lips. 'But I'm going 'round to her house after this and taking some comfort food. So, I'll take that cupcake.' She reached out for it, took it from Elizabeth's hand, wrapped it in the napkin Katy was offering, and deposited it in her fat shopping bag. 'It's all those little kids she teaches – they cough and sneeze all over her and she picks up their bugs.'

'That's just Kathryn,' chimed in Elizabeth, 'when she taught my sons she called them *her treasures*.' She looked sideways as if to see if anybody else could hear, 'I had other titles for them.'

Peter was slightly shocked by this. The yes-woman always spoke so kindly to everybody, he was trying to imagine what she called her sons.

'Since Kathryn's not here, there's something else I wanted to ask you all,' Anna said. Peter and Katy had gone back to their desks and the women were quietly sipping their hot drinks with their cupcakes. 'You know I've been having trouble with my landlord for a while?' They all nodded. 'He won't fix things around the unit and my lease is about to expire and he's putting up the rent. I think he wants me out, so he can refurbish it completely and get more money.'

'Do you want us to talk to him?' Di was practically pawing the ground – Anna could imagine her in full armour with a broadsword.

'No, that's not it.' Anna patted Di on the hand, 'But thank you. No. Kathryn has said she would like me to rent her spare room and come and live with her.'

There was a collective *Oh* from the group.

'What do you all think?' asked Anna

'Do you want to live with her?' enquired Elizabeth.

'I think it might work, and we could look after each other. We could share the housework to start with.'

'Do you have much stuff?' Patsy was ever practical.

'No, very little really, and some of it would go in the spare room and my table and chairs and fridge could be stored in her garage.'

'The two of you get on very well but you might both need a little space sometimes.' Di was reflecting on her own need for regular solitude.

'Sounds like you have it worked out,' Elizabeth said, 'so why would you like our advice?'

Anna shrugged. 'I have nobody else to discuss it with. And it's a big move. I've been on my own for so long. I guess it's just being with another person all day every day. Do you think I could do it?'

Katy had been quietly eavesdropping in her corner but suddenly broke out, 'If it doesn't work out, do you have a back-up plan? My nanna was a great one for a plan B.' She suddenly realised she had never mentioned her nanna to these women before – or Peter for that matter.

Anna nodded, 'My other choice is to find a new unit – probably not so close to here.'

There was silence as they all absorbed this. Elizabeth was nodding now, 'So why don't you say it's temporary for now and that you will look around for another place that suits. And if you enjoy living together, you can stay there, and if it doesn't work out you could move on without anybody being upset.' Well not too upset anyway, she thought to herself.

Anna stared down into her coffee cup, weighing up the idea, 'I think I'll try that. Thank you.' She beamed at them. 'I knew I could ask you all. You are such wise women.'

'And we could help you move,' said Katy, sweeping her arm to include Peter in the royal 'we'.

'Could we?' thought Peter, and then realised he had said it out loud when Katy answered him.

'Yes, we could, one Sunday. Just let us know when.'

Tears rolled down the lines on Anna's face. 'I knew you were family,' she said.

'Someday I'd like to go to Russia,' declared Katy one day when the sweet scent of blossom from the trees outside were giving the mall's

Lush a run for its money. Rather than giving them the old literature, she had recently been getting the women to help her come up with marketing strategies for the latest offers. A new batch of travel catalogues had come through the post and she was fanning them across the table for the Travel Club. The Russia tour was open before them and she was unconsciously stroking the full-page picture of the white and gold wedding cake of St. Petersburg's Winter Palace.

Kathryn and Anna walked through the door to find Elizabeth already seated.

'Why would you want to go there?' asked Anna, her eyes narrowed as the door closed silently behind her. She was remembering when the USSR dominated most of Europe, and the grim world behind the iron curtain that made men and women disappear.

'My nanna used to talk about Russia.' Katy was smiling at them but seeing her grandmother.

This Anna could understand. 'Was she a communist?' Kathryn narrowed her eyes at Anna as she spoke. They had been happily sharing the house now for a couple of months and talked about all sorts of things. She was still fascinated by Anna's life in Europe – although it was so long ago – but there were times when Anna would begin to speak about something, then stop – look away – and go on with another topic entirely. At first, Kathryn had worried that Anna was losing her memory, but lately she'd seen a pattern emerging: whenever Anna spoke about a particular group of friends, even if it was a funny story, she seemed to suddenly remember that this was off limits. It was as if she had been brainwashed. Perhaps they were communists. Kathryn hoped that a time would come when Anna could trust her with her secrets.

'No, not a communist – she used to say she didn't have a political bone in her body,' laughed Katy, and everybody caught the humour, 'a story teller. My dad called her an incurable romantic. Maybe she was, but she loved stories about old Russia.'

Anna wilted. 'You can't go back,' she said sadly.

In the silence Patsy, Di, and Kim came through the door and sat around the table. Anna had her head bowed, but the rest of the women gave her space and instead all eyed Katy expectantly.

'If you could choose anywhere in the world, where would you go?' asked Katy

'Vienna,' Kathryn and Anna spoke at once, and then laughed together and Kathryn realised that going to Vienna would indeed be going back for Anna. 'We would go to the opera, and lots of concerts and see the statue of the young Mozart in the Burggarten,' said Kathryn.

'And the Vienna Woods in blossom,' finished Anna. There was a collective sigh.

'Persia – I mean Iran,' Di said, giving Peter the eye across the room – which he patently ignored.

'London,' declared Kim.

Five heads snapped round to look at her, 'London?' they chorused.

'Well, I'd like to go back to Vietnam someday, but my daughter has moved to London for work and I would like to spend time with her there.' Kim had told them before about her youngest daughter who was a doctor and extending her specialist training.

'Too many wonderful places to choose from.' Elizabeth indicated all the posters around the walls. 'I'd just be happy to see any of them. What about you Patsy?' Elizabeth was looking at the top of Patsy's bowed head.

'Pity we can't time travel,' she finally replied, 'I'd like to go back and simply enjoy those good times when my husband was himself.'

The hard lump of grief Elizabeth had pushed down deep inside her suddenly rose up from her belly. 'Me too.' She patted her friend's hand, and the others looked away, bereft of words. It was like a gulf had opened and all their tears and fears were pulling them towards the abyss.

'Imagine,' from the other side of the shop, Katy's voice broke into the wall of memories, 'what it would mean for us if we could offer time travel as a new experience? Wow.'

Peter had got up and was looking at her as if she was possessed. The Six Sisters heads jerked up and they stared at her with their eyes like white dinner plates.

'Think of the marketing possibilities,' she added.

No thanks, thought Peter, I have enough trouble with the time I have. 'Have you ever thought,' he heard himself say, 'that tomorrow, today will be yesterday? And if we don't make the most of today we'll regret it tomorrow.' Where did that come from, he wondered. Had his mum said that to him? Maybe.

They were all looking at him speculatively. Eventually it was Patsy – of all people, he thought – who broke the air of stunned stupefaction: 'Quite right.' She drew herself up in the chair, pausing to form her scattered thoughts. 'So what I would like to say is – that although I'm not able to travel at present… one day,' and she drew a deep juddering breath, 'when the inevitable happens… and it won't be long now… and my darling is no longer in this world.' She swallowed to clear the thickening in her throat and Elizabeth put her arm around her. 'I would like to go and visit new places I've never been with him so I don't see him around every corner… and I hope it will be with all you lovely ladies.' Patsy considered the group and was surprised to see pale faces and eyes filled with tears.

Peter's gut tightened at the brave wisdom of her words. Then the thought jumped unbidden into his brain, what an opportunity – what a challenge – to take the Travel Club travelling. He looked at Katy over the top of Anna's head, and saw her black lips curve up into a pussycat grin. And his gut rolled upwards, grabbed his heart and shook it, screaming – what have you done?!

~ ELIZABETH ~

'After a long illness,' the death notice read. Patsy told me she thought for a long time about the words she would put in the paper. She had so much preparation time, after all. Do I envy her? Not really – watching him expire, inch by inch. But she had all those months to say what she wanted to her Ray. She used to get into bed with him at the nursing home. We all laughed when she told us that, but I was a bit shocked. I wondered what the nursing staff thought. She didn't really care. I know she was with him when he died. Holding him in those last moments as his breaths became less and less, like slow waves on a shallow sea, with oceans of time between. Did she tell him he was her heart and soul, and that her life would be half-lived without him? Did she kiss him full on the mouth, like young lovers do, and try to breathe for him? No opportunity. That's what I tell myself. I had no opportunity. Just that dreadful phone call from our young minister telling me they had found John slumped in front of the church computer – no breath, no pulse, no life. The minister, poor boy, had man-handled John to the floor in the small space between the desk and the door, and pumped away at his heart while his wife called the ambulance – and me. When I rushed in, the paramedics informed me it was sudden heart failure and they had done all they could – but it was too late. Too late. Too late for me to say all the things slammed tight in my heart. Too late to hold him one more time against my breast. Too late to breathe my life back into him.

Amazing how you keep going. You get up each morning and the sun's shining, or it's cloudy, or raining – it doesn't really matter. You wash, you eat, you shop as if life is going on – you smile, you talk to people, you make decisions – when half of you has vanished and only that practical part of your soul is working. So – what's worse – I ask myself – a long illness where you are systematically dismembered by their suffering, or sudden heart failure where the guillotine of grief falls swiftly?

There is no good answer. Only God knows. Both Patsy's and my hearts are sliced in two. But I am living proof you can exist with half a heart.

'How are the bookings looking?' asked Katy, waggling her pierced eyebrows at her rhyming. The women had all left and Peter had just sat down after lunch. Katy had been well trained not to ask men questions when they were hungry.

'Are you after a raise?' asked Peter carefully.

'Well,' she took a long breath, not wanting to admit he had caught her off-guard, and put her fingers to her lips thoughtfully, 'yes, that would be nice. I wouldn't turn one down.'

'Let me look into it.' He nodded, smiling at her restraint. 'But yes, we are doing better – and a lot of it's your hard work. So I will come up with something appropriate.'

'Not just my hard work,' she shook her head, 'yours too. And the Six Sisters have been raking in the money.'

This wasn't news to Peter. He had been forced to bring in more chairs. The regular meetings of the Travel Club sometimes had new people sitting around the table asking questions – or simply hanging out in the shop eavesdropping. The mall's bush telegraph seemed to be working overtime because he couldn't work out how anyone knew when to come. His tidy shop was replete with all sorts on the days the Six Sisters met, and people were coming back and booking holidays. And the travel companies were starting to question how he got all his business – he'd been staying mum about that.

Guilt washed over him. A cup of something hot and a weekly sweet was hardly appropriate recompense for the work the women poured into his business. They came whenever he asked them in ones and twos and more, and handled his clients with care, compassion, and a practical wisdom that made clients believe they really needed that special experience only he could offer. And yet, he didn't think any of the women had sold a holiday to someone who couldn't afford it. Sometimes they came up with workable and breath-taking experiences that left him reeling. The latest development was scheduling appointments with the sisters for clients who had returned from their holidays and wanted to discuss them. And those clients were bringing their friends in! It was all very jolly – and his profits were climbing weekly.

'I've been thinking,' ventured Katy.

Uh-oh, thought Peter, this sounded dangerous.

'We should start putting some money into a separate account called The Travel Club. And maybe we could help the Six Sisters achieve some of their dreams.'

Peter felt the warmth rise from his belly to his throat. What a treasure this pink-haired, black-lipped person was turning out to be. Creative to her ebony fingertips and gold-hearted to boot. He found he liked her ideas of helping others. Was it inborn or learned, he wondered, not to want to grasp everything to your own breast? The need to share not just your days, but what you possessed as well? It was certainly growing in him like a golden balloon, welling his chest.

'What a good idea.' He said. 'I will have to discuss it with my other partners.' He considered what he would say. 'But if we put a percentage in from all the holidays they have helped us sell and see what we come up with, I think that would be reasonable.'

Katy nodded. 'And don't forget my raise. I have dreams, too.'

~ PETER ~

I'm trying to work out if I ever dreamed anything. People think running your own business must be the realisation of a dream, but for me it was just something I could do – a job. I moved around a lot after school and so studying travel and working in the industry seemed to flow on naturally.

I really never knew what I wanted to be. I had a friend at school who assured me from kindergarten she was going to be a doctor. It was all she talked about. In high school, she used to ruin our lunchtimes with gory medical stories. And she worked so hard at it even when things didn't go well. She was a paramedic at first and then went on to study medicine – she's a great doctor – she helped me so much with Mum. I used to think if I could just work out who I was, like she had, then I could be that thing – and be happy. But life's not so straight-forward.

When Mum had her stroke, it seemed natural for me, as the unmarried son, to be the carer. I'd come back briefly to help but my brother and sister both had families to care for and houses on the other side of the city. I didn't mind staying home; my itchy feet were temporarily stilled. I loved Mum. Even when times were hard, we got on well. And the local travel agent gave me some casual work and at the end let me work from home, so we still had some income. There really wasn't time to dream. Who would have thought Mum could have lived ten years like that? So incapacitated and dependant – and furious at herself to be like that. The only time I had away from her was when I went shopping or went for my run first thing in the morning. Mum kept urging me to go out. Ask somebody on a date. 'Who,' I'd say. 'Anybody,' she'd retort. But while I was roaming the world, most of my friends married and moved on and there was little opportunity to meet new people. I settled into a comfortable rut while I helped sell adventures to other folk. In the end, it was cancer that took her. A rapid onset and a peaceful end, flying high on morphine. And I found that tough too – having those one-way conversations with her frozen, fading face. My brother and sister and all the family gathered around in the last week to take turns in sitting by Mum's comatose form – but I felt guilty when I was away from her.

I took a holiday when it was over. Went on a cruise to the Pacific Islands. Blue skies, creamy beaches, alcohol laid on. Fun, fun, fun. Relaxing. Inert. Empty. It seemed as if the shell of me was on the boat and all my bleeding viscera were back in Mum's stuffy bedroom. When I returned, the family decided I needed a job and we would pool our money and invest in the local travel agency that was for sale. Simple really, no dreams required…

CHAPTER FIVE

As summer came in, the Travel Club welcomed two new visitors. They had been told for some weeks that Peter had a surprise for them and they'd all been giving it their best guess.

'Do you think he has a woman?' asked Anna, when Peter had ducked out to buy some more morning tea.

'Does he need one?' Di speculated.

They all looked at her. No, surely not. You could hear the humming in the air.

'Every man needs a woman. Mostly to clean and cook and find lost things,' laughed Kim. 'Although he's very tidy. Maybe he manages,' she added

Katy was having a quiet laugh in the corner. She'd been privy to other conversations where the Six Sisters had been planning a match for Peter.

'Let him look after his own life,' said Patsy, 'we all get to choose.'

Some things we get to choose, some choose us, thought Elizabeth, but could not say it.

'Is Kathryn coming?' she said instead to Anna.

Anna nodded. 'Yes, but she has a student. She asked me to say she'll be a little late.'

'How's the living together?' asked Di.

'Good, I think, still temporary.' Anna smiled, 'but I'm not looking very hard for anything else.'

Katy was thinking about the day she and Peter had helped Anna move. There was so little to take across to Kathryn's place. Peter had turned up in T-shirt and jeans, an ancient trailer hooked to the back of his car. One load was all they needed to move the furniture across the suburb. The contrast could not have been more stark: Anna's sparsely furnished, bare-walled, one-bedroom unit, compared to Kathryn's elegant family home, furnished with antique furniture and walls covered in photos of relatives and of young Kathryn, when she travelled the world as a concert pianist. Peter and Katy had stowed the plain table and two chairs in the back room with the sun pouring in where Kathryn assured Anna they were just the thing to eat breakfast off on winter mornings. In went the bed to the empty bedroom Kathryn had cleared and Katy winced at how Anna's meagre belongings took so little space in the immense room. Katy had lived all her life with Nanna and Dad's stuff and found it difficult to imagine how anyone could possess so little. But she noticed that it made no difference to Kathryn or Anna. They were friends, and that was that.

She was interrupted from her musings by Peter ushering a man and a woman through the door to the agency. Surprisingly he locked the door behind him, then, when there was an immediate rap on the glass, had to turn around and let Kathryn in.

'Sorry, sorry,' he apologised, 'I didn't want us to be interrupted.' He smiled at Katy and then the women. 'Let me introduce you to my associates. This is my sister, Carol and my brother, David. We're all partners in this business.' Surprise and dismay warred across the women's faces.

'It's okay everybody.' Katy had risen to her feet and was shaking hands with Peter's siblings in a surprisingly adult manner. She turned to the women. 'It's good news, not bad.' A collective *Ahhhh* came back at her. 'Did you bring the extra morning tea?' she asked Peter. He nodded. 'Then let's get down to business.'

It was Carol and David's turn to look surprised. This elf girl was giving their brother instructions and he seemed to be enjoying it. In fact, for the first time they could remember, he was smiling, and his blue-green eyes were sparkling with excitement. Welcome back, Carol thought, to the land of the living.

There were introductions all round and, while Katy and Peter served tea, coffee and the excellent fruit flan from the patisserie, the women talked a little about themselves and particularly how they had become so interested in travel. Carol and David grew more and more impressed with the group that Peter referred to as the Travel Club. They were so well spoken, erudite and downright inspiring. His siblings could understand why people wanted to hear their stories because they could imagine sitting here every week entranced by exotic tales of foreign shores.

When everybody was settled, munching and sipping away, Peter finally got down to talking business. 'I wanted you to meet my partners – well, really, my family – before I told you about this, so you'd know it's not just some hare-brained, impossible scheme I dreamt up.' He smiled at the women, who were rapt. 'Our business here has improved so much that we've decided to put aside a reasonable percentage of the profits from the holidays the Travel Club sells so that you can all enjoy travelling. We want you to live your own dreams.'

He was greeted with a wall of silence. For a moment, he thought he had made a very serious error that would forever alter the delicate beauty of the relationship he shared with these women. Then Anna burst into tears.

'Can I travel to Vienna and meet my son?' she sobbed.

As if one surprise wasn't enough, thought Peter. Katy had both hands glued to her lips. The other women's mouths were wide open in perfect o-rings like carollers on a Christmas card. He hoped nobody had a heart attack, the defibrillator was down the other end of the mall.

Kathryn was the first to recover. She stood up, walked around behind Anna in the chair and bent down, folding her friend in her arms. Explanations could wait, she thought, 'Of course you can.' She looked sideways at Peter and he nodded.

There was a collective sigh and the whole room was nodding with him. Peter felt his head bobbing up and down, leading the head-dance. He could feel his thoughts bouncing around inside like balls in a bingo barrel – he was standing outside himself, waiting to see who would win – his logical brain or that surging heart that was longing to give Anna her dearest wish.

~ ANNA ~

If I'd known a little more and loved a little less, my life would have been – well, I don't really know what my life would have been without Hans. We were both sixteen and studying at the Conservatory. I accompanied his soulful violin and we did make marvellous music together. In this day you couldn't conceive that anybody would know so little about conception.

I had spent my girlhood incarcerated at the school where the nuns hinted darkly at "what bad girls did" and my mother was very reticent about anything she deemed "too personal", so I really had no idea what Hans and I were doing. He assured me it was normal and as natural as it was exciting. Filled with adrenalin after a concert, we'd fall into one another's arms for our own performance. When I stopped menstruating and started to fill out, I was astonished to hear I was pregnant.

My father spoke to Hans' family and their response was to move him to another music school in another country. My mother wouldn't speak to anybody in the family, least of all me – her musical golden child who had turned to dross. She did, however, speak to her priest, who informed the nuns, and they took me very firmly into their bat-like clutches and only released me when I had born my son and given him over to them for adoption. There was no question about any alternative. I came home to find there was no home left. My mother remained silent as stone, looking out the window, over the snowy streets, to a seemingly rosy place. My father suggested kindly that I might like to emigrate and start a new life. Even as I left

Vienna forever, mother did not share one word with me, nor ever wrote back to me until the day she died.

Who did I miss more? My son? I hardly saw him. I managed to get one quick glance at him as he came out of me and then the nuns held up a sheet. Hans? We never spoke again. He became a concert violinist and I heard he'd died in a plane crash in his late twenties. My mother? Why would she blame me for something she should have told me about? My father? The day I left he folded me in his arms, whispering lovingly, 'Don't come back, there is no-one here for you now.' In this way, I was robbed of the opportunity to grieve over any loss. I did, in time, grow to hate whining violins.

CHAPTER SIX

'That went well,' said Carol, sipping her mineral water in the pub on the corner opposite the mall.

'Did it?' David was looking at her sideways. 'I think our Pete could've bitten off more than he can chew.' He glanced at his brother who was gulping down his beer like it was his last drink.

They had invited Katy along to talk to her about her raise and taking on more responsibility in the agency. She had been hesitant to speak up but was feeling a bit sorry for her boss. 'It *will* be fine,' she assured them, 'we *can* make it happen.'

'Do you think that European woman might be too old to travel?' continued David. Peter's face was buried in his beer.

'How old is she?' Carol was trying to slow David down a bit.

'In her late seventies,' said Katy, who knew this from the surveys.

David was shaking his head.

Peter thumped the empty schooner down on the wooden table, sending the coasters skittering across the polished wooden surface. 'She's not too old and I *am* going to make it happen.'

Carol and David's eyes were wide with astonishment, Katy was wearing her pussycat smile, her insides glowing with pride.

'Now let's talk to Katy about that raise.'

A couple of hours at the pub and they had come up with a plan. Katy would take on more tasks in recognition of the raise and find somebody to work part time to do some of the clerical duties she hated. Peter was going to be more of a manager, and less hands on. He would also spend more time with the Travel Club and come up with a plan for them.

Just before they left, Carol asked if her son Justin could come and do some work experience. He was at a loose end and didn't know what he wanted to do in his future, and Carol thought this might help. Peter was caught between the rock of family and the hard place of Justin's attachment to his mobile phone. 'Yes,' he said, 'but,' he added, and Carol and David both looked at him, 'he has to turn off his technology.'

Katy was laughing under her breath, she had learned this very early in her job – no social media, no phone unless it was for work – this might be fun. Meanwhile, she was in charge of finding herself an assistant.

Peter's fascination with Katy's interviewing techniques kept him endlessly amused. Of course, he didn't laugh out loud in front of her. Instead, he had taken to reliving them at home after work and breaking up in the privacy of his own kitchen as he got dinner. Her list of questions went something like this:

Have you travelled yourself?
What star sign are you?
If you could go anywhere in Australia, where would it be?
What's your favourite colour?
If you could go anywhere in the world where would you go?
What do you like for morning tea?
Where have you worked before and what did you do?

These could be in any order and elicited some astonished looks and surprising responses. If she asked about work, first there were quite a few outlandish statements – experts in their fields – you would think. Peter couldn't help but wonder why somebody would want a part time job as a clerical assistant when they thought they were so important. If, however, Katy asked what he considered to be alternative questions first, she sometimes managed to soften up the interviewee so that the truth spilled out of them like froth from a cappuccino. So, he got over his initial hesitation and started to see it as her plan.

When he shared his faith in her sneakiness, it was her turn to be astonished.

'Outrageous questions,' she choked. 'Outrageous! Do you want to work with somebody with a star sign that will clash with yours?'

He reflected that he didn't even know his own star sign, so he found it difficult to envisage a cosmic war in the agency.

'Or if they wear outfits that don't blend in with the décor.' She swept her hand around, joyfully ignoring the clash between her bright halo of hair and myriad of piercings and the exotic towns laid out on the white walls behind her.

Maybe, he mused, she did fit into the decorating plan in a neo-medieval way. Hang on, he thought, before her he'd never had a plan – just stick the pictures on the walls and hope for the best. Now he could see an order in the walls, as if you were walking down a time-tunnel into a distant future. Was he losing it entirely?

'What if they're gluten free?' he snapped back to reality as she raced on. 'How will the Travel Club cope with that?' She was building up a head of steam. 'You know they expect everybody to join in. How will they survive if the person doesn't eat cake?'

'Let them eat cake.' He murmured, trying to bite his tongue but out it came anyway and evoked a cynical smile in response.

'Exactly,' she replied, and stared at her screen. Did she know about Marie Antoinette, he wondered, was she suggesting a revolution?

When she made her final decision to offer the job, it surprised Peter completely. Despite most applicants being women, Katy chose an older man named Bob. He had spent his career in middle management, and Peter thought rather uncharitably he still carried the management around his middle and would indeed eat cake. He was semi-retired by necessity as the firm where he had spent his career had gone into receivership. Finding life at home boring, he decided to look for any job that would give him a little income and a reason to get out of bed in the morning. He had applied for lots of full-time jobs and been told he was too old – so he was up for anything.

When Katy had asked him his star sign, he had admitted that he didn't know what it was but if she was worried about it, he could find out. He also said that he tried to avoid personality clashes, be nice to everybody and just get on with the job. 'Learnt that by being in the middle,' said Bob, 'do your job properly and if you don't know what to do, ask. I'm happy to do anything you need around the office, run errands for you and I know a bit about computers, so I can help with that if you need it.' He was also interested in travel and happy to read up on anything that looked like fun.

'I think he'll be perfect,' said Katy. 'He's travelled a bit and so knows that side of the business – and he is really nice.' She smiled and nodded encouragingly at Peter, so what could he say? Since he had been out when Katy conducted that particular interview, they got Bob in for a second chat and then offered him the job. Two days a week and one of those would be when the Travel Club met.

~ BOB ~

There were several things I didn't tell Katy during that interview – not exactly lies, just missing pieces in the jigsaw of my life. One of those empty spaces was my family life – or lack thereof. Once, I'd been a happily married man with a pigeon pair, a cat, a dog, a goldfish and a moderate mortgage. Well, I'd considered myself happy but evidently my wife not so much. When the children were about to leave home, she announced that she was also fleeing the nest. Moving out with a girlfriend – and I found out later she was actually a girlfriend in the most intimate sense – taking the cat and the dog with her – she'd never cared for the goldfish. I remembered the knife in my gut – the sheer disbelief when confronted with her words. Never happy, I thought, never – never – never. I remember asking the goldfish, how could two people live together for over twenty years and not know what the other was thinking – or doing for that matter – or even who they were doing it with?

Nobody at my old work was included in this secret. I kept the visceral hole in my soul covered with the genial image of a well-fed husband and a loving dad. When I had to sell our house and move into an apartment, I let it be known that, with the children off our hands, we were down-sizing. My children were nonplussed. They, it appeared, had also been happy and presumed the stable home their parents offered was a stable for everybody. By this time, my wife was letting loose all the animosity hidden beneath that unyielding busyness.

'Was it lack of love,' my daughter asked at that final gathering of the clan.

'Not exactly,' my wife replied, 'I'm still very fond of your father.' My stomach still roils at the echo of her patronising tone.

'Then why?' our son pressed.

'I just want more.' My wife was looking at me and I shrank down in my favourite armchair as she pinned me there with her glare. She took a deep breath and said, 'Do you know I never had an orgasm with your father – not once.' And with that she got up, seized the rest of her two decades worth of belongings and left the building. I stayed nailed to that chair for hours, my whole being shredded.

Eventually my red-faced son and daughter departed as well, not knowing whose side to take – their recently emboldened mother or their newly eviscerated father.

The Six Sisters took Bob to their collective bosom like a long-lost son. That is to say they gently corrected his mistakes, fed him as he served them morning tea, loaded him up with their shopping bags to go to the carpark, and grilled him like the Spanish Inquisition. Bob loved every minute of it.

'How's he going, do you think?' Peter asked Katy as she sat down to work one quiet Monday morning.

'What? Who?'

'Bob, who else?'

'Well it could be anybody else.' She grinned sideways at him, the piercing in her right eyebrow waggling winsomely. 'You could be asking me about the Prime Minister. Dad said he's not going so well. Still – dad doesn't like anybody in parliament – it's part of his religion to hate all the parties. He says it doesn't matter who you elect, you always get a politician.'

Peter drew breath but before he could speak she continued, 'Or you could be talking about that bloke on the radio that's in so much trouble, I'm sick of hearing about him.' She was still going, 'or my favourite heavy metal singer, or my boyfriend.'

'You have a boyfriend?' Peter's mouth was in gear before his brain – way too personal.

'Well… no. But if I did have a boyfriend… It's not my fault. Nothing wrong with me.' Her face matched her hair.

'Of course, there's not – you're fine,' said Peter, and surprisingly, he believed it. The muscles in her face relaxed instantly. 'So,' continued Peter, 'how is Bob going?'

'I think he lends an air of professionalism to the agency.'

Peter's brows climbed to his hairline. Was that a dig at him? He nodded at Katy to continue.

She smiled, 'He always comes to work in a tie and coat.'

Peter hated wearing a tie and thought a clean company shirt sufficed.

'He addresses clients as sir and madam,' she added

Peter had to give her that point.

'And it makes them feel valued.' She thought carefully. 'Are sales up?'

'Slightly.'

'Well there you go.' She looked out through the glass door, as she chose her words carefully, 'and I think he builds on the Travel Club's efforts.' She shuffled her wheelie chair across to his desk and, leaning forward towards him, switched subjects with a flick of her hair.

'What's the plan for Anna to meet her son?'

'It's coming along,' he answered as he backed up on his squeaky chair like a truck in a loading dock.

'I didn't ask how the planning was coming, I asked what the actual plan is.' She wheeled forward as he retreated towards the wall.

'I'm working on it.'

'What have you done?'

'This and that.' He was not sure where to begin really.

'Tell me about "this".' She was having none of his evasion this morning.

'I have a list,' he said, scooting around her back to his computer and making her retreat with a screech of wheels: 'There.'

She peered at his list:

It said 'To Do' in big letters

> *Air fares*
> *Accommodation*
> *Insurance*
> *Passports*
> *Who is going?*
> *Where are we going?*
> *How long will we stay?*
> *Where else will we visit?*

'What's with the "we"?' said Katy

'I thought I might take them.'

'So, you think there will be more than one? Who else?'

'Well, Kathryn for a start – and possibly Elizabeth. Maybe some of the others.'

'Who's going to look after the agency?'

It was his turn to smile. 'Why, you of course. And Bob could work full time while I'm away.'

Wow, she thought, maybe I'll get another raise. She tried to look suitably business-like. 'Okay, now tell me about "that". Do you know where you're going yet?'

A sheepish smile creased his face. 'Not really. We need to know more about Anna's story but I'm too scared to ask – I don't want to make her cry again.'

That made sense, her father was also a scaredy-cat when it came to womanly tears – as she'd sometimes used to her advantage. Would they work on Peter? That was worth consideration.

She smiled back at him. 'Maybe I could ask.' Then she thought again. 'On second thoughts, what about Bob? They say all sorts of things to him. He seems to have the knack.'

'What a good idea.' Peter breathed a sigh of relief. Easy to make decisions about job allocations when the person wasn't in the room.

'Now,' said Katy, 'Let me help you with that list.'

~ PATSY ~

The garden's a mess. Couch grass everywhere set like concrete by the dry summer. Weeds pretending to be flowers and all the vegetables run to seed. Long months visiting Ray and I never even noticed how overgrown it'd become until this morning. Like somebody switched the light back on. At least my neighbours have been taking it in turns to mow the lawns. Eden, was what we called our garden, and like Adam and Eve we were equally unaware of the pain we could feel outside our sanctuary. And now I am cast out into this wilderness that used to be my paradise.

Maybe I should leave it like this – a symbol of my thinking, my living, my loving. Somehow, I've lost touch with order – drifted off into a waving wasteland of weeds. Perhaps a list would help. I could write down what I plan to do and then put it into action – it worked before – I used to make lists for Ray. He called them his cattle dogs – never could say catalogues – and besides, my demands rounded him up for work. No point going down that path, it brings terrible inertia. It's like I'm floundering face-forward into a black hole – which is probably the future. Perhaps first thing on my list should be finding who I am – alone. I always loved to travel –

maybe now I'll have the chance to go and discover what I have become.

The late afternoon sun spilled through the stained-glass fanlights along Patsy's back door and trickled through the pale hair of the four women seated around the table. Bob reached out for another chicken sandwich and saw his hand pass through the spectrum, the bread shifting shades through a nebula of scarlet, blue and yellow as he slowly lifted it to his mouth. Redemption was the promise of the rainbow, he was thinking to himself – and how the women resembled saints, haloed by the coronas of colour.

Patsy had been in discussions with him about her joining Anna and Kathryn on their journey and Bob had told her of the need to know more. Simple, exclaimed Patsy, and arranged a high tea. They could all come along and bare their souls. Just like confession, she joked, but with Tim Tams. Then she started to worry because she didn't know whether Bob was Catholic – she may have offended him. He seemed happy today though, charming all the ladies. Hard to tell, he always appeared so calm and friendly.

Anna was telling them all about her son, Michael. She had received a letter from him six months ago, asking questions to determine if she was his mother. A photo was included, and that sealed the truth for Anna.

'He could not have been anybody else. I began to dream I was coming back and my father was welcoming me.'

The women were all nodding their encouragement, the colours shifting up and down highlighting their hairdos.

'He has had a good life, he tells me, and a good education – he's an engineer. His parents were kind to him and he's been happily married for a long time.' She swallowed deeply, then sighed. 'I have grandchildren and great-grandchildren. The youngest grandson is a musician.' Tears rolled down the creases either side of her nose. 'A whole family, I have, and I never knew.'

Kathryn put her strong, warm hand over Anna's and squeezed. There were no words she could find to comfort her friend. Elizabeth poured more tea and coffee.

'How wonderful,' said Bob. 'What a blessing.' They all looked at him. He kept very quiet about his personal life.

'Have a Tim Tam,' Patsy passed the plate, 'and tell us about your family.'

And suddenly in that rainbow-drowned cathedral of a room, Bob's mouth opened, and his memories overflowed like a dam in flood. He told them all about his son and daughter, his seemingly happy home, and how his wife had left him for another woman. Gradually, his broken heart began to throb again. In fact, it was racing.

'Do you see your children?' asked Elizabeth.

'Oh, yes. On Father's Day and my birthday… Sometimes… at Christmas.' He thought for a bit. 'Well, not every year, but they often ring me at those times. In fact, a couple of weeks ago I went to my new grandson's naming day.' He smiled beneficently, feeling he had finally reached a positive point regarding his family.

'Was your wife there too?' Patsy turned to him with her head on one side. Bob's stomach felt like a millstone had dropped in it.

His smile drooped. 'Of course.'

'With her partner?' Elizabeth asked.

He nodded disconsolately and then picked himself up. 'A wonderful woman,' it came out all in one breath, 'my children love her, and she makes my ex-wife very happy.'

'And you did not?' Anna's quiet European voice slashed through his last reserves.

He shook his head and stared at the diminishing plate of Tim Tams. 'Apparently not. She said she had never enjoyed…' He thought carefully about his words as the heat rose up the back of his neck, '… our marriage. Told our children she had never had a… a…' He was struggling to say the word, 'a… *climax*… with me.' He could feel the blood starting to rise up his cheeks. What on earth had made him say that? He stared harder at the Tim Tams. They looked traditional, but you never really knew with all these flavours Arnott's tried – the Turkish Delight had been good. Maybe these were Spill-Your-Guts Tim Tams.

'She probably wouldn't know an orgasm if it got up and bit her,' Kathryn said with a mouth full of chocolate biscuit.

When the shock of hearing her speak of sex in a thick QM voice had passed, the silence was shattered by their laughter.

'I'm sure it's not your fault. She was probably always gay and didn't know it,' Kathryn added.

Elizabeth was thinking that the wife could have said it privately, and not in front of their children, and soon found those very words issuing from her mouth.

The redness rushed across Bob's face like a windy sunset. There was a general nod of agreement around the table. Kathryn also found herself wondering what Patsy had put in the afternoon tea that provoked such frankness – and glanced out at the overgrown herbs in the garden.

'Welcome to the club, Bob,' smiled Patsy.

Bob felt his insides relax.

'We all have difficult things in our past.' She took a deep breath thinking that perhaps a change of subject was in order. 'I've decided I'd like to come on the journey with you. I think Ray would want me to.' She rose and went into the other room, returning with a writing pad and a pen. 'So, let's decide what we need to do to make this happen.'

'A list,' declared Elizabeth, 'I love a list.'

~ KIM ~

I am so caught between two loves – stretched out like an octopus drying in the sun. I love going to the Travel Club; it fills my days and makes my heart light. This is the first time I have had such close friends in Australia and I am so happy when I am with them it's like being back in my girlhood again. We talk about everything – where we have been, who we were with, the funny things that happened, the sadness that changed our lives, the loves we left behind.

But of course, my great love is still with me. My husband listens carefully when I talk about my new friends, and gently reminds me that we have travelled in the past and are happy and secure here. I just want to say – let's go again for fun this time, before it's too late. Let's enjoy ourselves. He is happy and safe among our family – and so am I, but I want to live life like a banquet, enjoying every day without fear. We are *citizens, we* can *get passports, we* can *come back, and nobody can say go away, I have told him. But still he doesn't want to.*

I watch Elizabeth and Patsy, so sad, trying so hard to find a new life, and I'm grateful I still have him. But I also wish I could do as I please. So here I am, strung out with no idea of how to be free.

Justin arrived in the agency in late November with a severe case of the end-of-year I-can't-be-thereds. He slunk through the door one warm morning like a lizard round a fence post.

Katy looked up. 'Can I help you?' She found herself talking to a woolly fringe over a mobile phone.

'Huh?' His head flipped back, and she was struck by his brown teddy-bear eyes.

Peter was coming through the glass door slightly behind him. 'Hello, Justin.' Peter sighed as Justin hastily stowed his phone in his back pocket. 'Come to work, have you?'

'Work!?' Giggles threatened to explode out of Katy's dark lips – this might make her days very interesting. Justin was staring at her, taking in the matching black mouth and nails, and her iridescent hair. Fire Truck, it was called, and Peter had said something like that to himself when he first saw it. But, like most of Katy's eccentricities, it had grown on him.

She grinned and beckoned Justin over to the spare wheelie chair. 'Come and sit down,' she smiled seductively, 'and tell me what you like to do.'

Justin walked slowly forward in a hypnotic blur and Peter's stomach fell like a disconnected elevator and then rose again. She has a plan, he thought. Just as well, because he didn't.

'Who's the boy?' asked Kim, as she caught a glimpse of Justin photocopying out the back.

'Justin,' said Peter

'His nephew,' Katy added.

'He doesn't look like you,' Elizabeth put in. Peter had never considered this, not really expecting his siblings' children to bear any of his traits. Where Peter was tall and blue eyed with dirty blond hair, Justin was olive skinned with dark hair and eyes. Peter suddenly noticed his nephew was almost his height now. He wordlessly shook his head at Elizabeth.

Justin came back out into the shopfront as the Travel Club was seating themselves around the table.

'Justin – put the photocopying over there,' said Katy, indicating the table around which the women had perched themselves, 'and then you can ask them who would like tea and who would like coffee.'

This was a revelation to Justin. He had seen himself as a high-flying travel agent, selling worldly locations to wealthy clients. He looked at his uncle, who pursed his lips and nodded in agreement. Tea and coffee for a bunch of old women? Then he remembered his mother's threat. He was supposed to do whatever Uncle Peter wanted or she would cut the power plug off the Xbox. So, he smiled politely and asked each of the women separately what they would like. Then, ferrying the morning tea backwards and forwards, he tried not to spill the hot drinks.

Peter, mouth sagging, was watching his nephew satisfy each

individual order. He looked at Katy, who was working at her computer, and she smiled like a cat over the top of the screen and waggled the piercings on her eyebrows at him. He glanced across the room to where Bob was also concentrating completely on his screen and noticed that the man's belly was shaking with suppressed laughter. Not just him then. They were all sharing the joke. That felt very matey. He thought of taking Justin aside and showing him how to make a list of the teas and coffees, or even count them on his fingers and then decided that this was much more fun. Behind him, he heard Katy cough gently to attract his attention.

He turned to her and her eyes sparked with mirth. 'Would you like to start now?' she asked him.

He was momentarily confused.

'Are we going to talk about the trip? And what they will need?'

He was coming back to the point.

'Passports and so on?' she asked.

'Ah, yes,' he said, and nearly fell about again, as Justin tripped over a chair leg staring into the wobbling coffee cup. 'The trip. Who's going?'

'We are,' chorused Anna and Kathryn, then laughed.

'I am,' stated Elizabeth, smiling.

'Me too,' Patsy added, 'maybe I could share with you?' She looked at Elizabeth, who nodded slowly.

'I'm not sure,' said Di, making everyone look sideways, 'I may have something else I need to do.'

'Ah, a mystery.' Kathryn was smiling at her. 'Sounds exciting.'

Di relaxed. 'I'll let you know, when I know.'

They were all looking at Kim. 'I want to,' she said softly, 'but I don't want to go without my husband. And I don't think he wants to leave Australia.' Her unhappy face turned to look up into Justin's eyes as he put her tea in her hand.

'Why wouldn't he want to leave Australia?' he said and the whole room held its collective breath.

Kim's head was gently moving from side to side. 'It was so hard for us to come here. So many bad things happened. We nearly didn't get here.' She stared down into her china cup. 'We nearly died. Others did.' Her head suddenly came up and her dark eyes were fixed straight on Peter's. 'And he loves this country so much, I think he is afraid to leave it.'

'Would he come to the Travel Club?' asked Bob. 'Maybe I could talk to him.'

The room breathed again.

'I'll ask him,' she said, 'and if he won't come here, maybe you could all come and visit us. You could come for Sunday lunch.'

'What a lovely idea,' Katy was smiling at all of them, 'We'd love to.'

Justin found himself caught up in the moment. 'Me too?' Where did that come from, he wondered?

His uncle was equally surprised. Did Justin know he wouldn't get paid on a Sunday? Maybe it was the promise of food. All that growing, he mused, and tried to remember if he had eaten so much when he was a teenager.

Kim switched her shy smile to Justin. 'Of course, you too. We would love you to come.'

Katy tapped Justin on the shoulder, 'Why don't you go down to the bakery and buy something nice for morning tea. I'll finish the drinks.' She gave him some money and pushed him out the door. Just in time, she realised, as everybody broke up in laughter.

'He's on a steep learning curve,' Kathryn said.

'It's good for him.' Bob could see the potential in the boy. 'That's why we introduced him to you ladies – you can train him.'

'What a challenge,' laughed Kathryn.

'What a privilege,' said Elizabeth. And their laughter turned to solemn nods.

Once they got down to business, it became obvious to Peter that it would take some time to organise this trip. Only Kathryn and Elizabeth had passports, the others would need time, assistance, and know-how to apply for them. Then there was where to go. Katy had suggested to Kim that her husband might come if they included London in their itinerary, so they could visit their daughter. She was aware that this was a long way from Vienna, but it was still in Europe. The women went away with their photocopied lists of places and possibilities to think over and left Justin with plenty to think about that didn't involve social media – or maybe it could.

~ PETER ~

The agency used to be my man cave. A refuge where I could vicariously travel the world and make just enough to pay the rent and eat. Here I am now with a bird of paradise as an assistant, a part-time professional as a researcher, paying one of the Mario Brothers for work experience, and the Six Sisters teaching us all new tricks. Luckily, the agency is bringing in enough to support the circus. Am I the ring master? Maybe, but I have the feeling that the ring is controlling the master.

What possessed me to decide to take the women overseas? Am I soft? Mum used to say I was a born carer. I accepted her gratitude but now I wonder if she meant more than providing her care. I'm finding the truth that I really am happiest when I'm making other people happy. I think I learned that in Scouts once. Baden Powell said it, if I remember correctly. Scouts used to be my refuge when I was a kid and it also gave me wanderlust.

All those years ago, roaming alone was exciting, but when I think back, it felt like I was never connected and never content. Here with my travelling circus I find myself anticipating each day, enjoying the company and sleeping soundly of a night. Katy has become such a help to me and now I see beyond the outrageous clothes and make up and I look forward to everything she brings to my life. Justin is smitten with her and I see him falling over himself – literally sometimes – to please her. Where on earth are we all going to land?

CHAPTER SEVEN

On the late summer day when the latest *Travel Europe* magazine came in, the circus was shattered. Bob had taken to combing through magazines looking for new experiences to offer clients. He liked to share his titbits with whoever had ears to hear. The Travel Club relished these dissertations because they loved him chatting to them. He was smart enough to realise that by filtering the information through the women's wisdom, he could come up with unusual experiences and exciting possibilities particularly suitable for retirees. Passing them on to clients then involved an invitation to one or more of the Six Sisters to expand the offer to include all sorts of fun, way past his ideas.

The agency was quiet. Justin had gone home early for a school function and the shopping centre echoed like an empty silo. Bob had finished all his tasks and was tidying up the shopfront when he came across the magazine. Sitting down, his legs sagging under him, he started leafing through the glossy pages. A familiar face caught his attention. Di was staring back at him, her mouth curved in a fetching smile, and below it was a column entitled "Tales from Old Europe".

'Look at this, it's one of the sisters.' He held up the magazine, and Peter and Katy's heads jerked up like synchronised swimmers.

'Wow,' said Katy, 'that might be why she can't go on the trip.'

'I knew she wrote for a living. I thought it was mainly trade magazines.' Peter rose from his chair and, walking across the room, took the magazine from Bob's outstretched hands. Down the deserted corridors of the mall, Katy could hear footsteps resounding like heartbeats. She was watching Peter's face, which had turned from smiling at the portrait to a grieved grimace.

'What's wrong?' she was rising out of her chair.

Peter was shaking his head. 'No, no, no. She can't do this. She *cannot* do this.'

'What's she done?' Bob asked.

Peter could not answer. He just kept repeating himself. 'No, no, no.'

Katy detached the magazine from Peter's quaking hands and pressed him down onto the seat. He sat there obediently, hands held tight together between his spread knees, head rotating back and forth like a weather vane in a cool change. She read, very cautiously, down through the column, her bright hair flaming under the neon light. Finally, she lowered the pages and looked at the men, 'She's sharing the personal stories of the Travel Club.'

'Can she do that?' asked Bob

'She already has,' Peter whispered.

Katy put her black-nailed hands softly on each man's shoulder. 'Let's think about this,' she said, 'and then we'll talk to the rest of the sisters.'

Justin had just managed to live through a hellish week, he was only allowed to come and work on Saturday because his mother could now see his bedroom floor. Admittedly, some of his stuff was under the bed but he'd pulled the cover well down to hide it. He considered the home front as his civil war. All the way across the city on the swaying train he sat hunched over his phone, playing the latest Mario Brothers game, while on another level he replayed the latest battles with his parents. Still alive, he thought, as the carriage lurched back and forth and the woman standing next to him nearly landed in his lap.

He looked up and realised that she was not young. In fact, she reminded him a bit of Elizabeth, the yes-woman, Uncle Peter fondly called her. For the first time in his whole short life, Justin knew just what to do. He turned off the game, put his phone in his pocket, unbent his long legs to the vertical, tapped the lady on the shoulder and said, 'Would you like a seat, ma'am?' He'd learned that last word from Bob. It always worked for him.

The lady's head jerked in surprise, then her eyes lit up and she nodded. 'Thank you so much. My knees aren't very good at standing in a moving vehicle anymore.' She sighed as she plonked down on the vinyl train seat and peered back up at him. 'Your mother must be proud of you. You're such a gentleman.'

He wanted to say, could I have that in writing please? So, I can show Mum. But he just smiled and nodded, and his insides started to loosen a little. He found, without the Mario Brothers to distract him, his feet dancing to the rhythm of the train, he was going over the conversations to the click-clack on the rails.

It had all started when they had parent-teacher interviews. You would have thought his parents would know what to expect, but apparently not. They believed he was going to be a rocket surgeon – well maybe not – but at least get into some sort of uni course. Why, he'd asked, when his parents had come fuming into the house, should I want to go to uni? Uncle Peter doesn't have a degree, and he's successful. He could have swallowed his tongue as soon as he said it, the black look on his father's face. Maybe, said his father, but you're not him, you're my son and I expect more from you. You need to work harder at school. And, his mother put in, you need to work harder at home too – then, of course, the bedroom came up. Why was tidiness so important to them? After all, it was his room, he had to live in it. He guessed it was their house. Or was it his? That would be a difficult conversation with his parents. He'd rather be at the agency than anywhere. Everybody there seemed to care about him and not make life hard. Not like at home where he was always in the gun.

He opened the shop-front door feeling more light-hearted, and then the atmosphere inside struck him down like a cricket bat. Wow, he thought, what's going on here – uh-oh I'm in trouble again.

Katy, looked up at him, the frown creasing her forehead slipping into a smile, just for him, he thought, and she patted the seat next to her. 'Come over here and I'll tell you our news. Maybe you can help us sort out this problem.'

Me, he thought, they want me to help, ME. 'Certainly ma'am,' he said, and donned his thinking cap.

~ JUSTIN ~

If I was Anna, would I be upset? Not sure. People say all sorts of things these days on social media. They even put up pics of themselves doing stuff – and that doesn't include sexting. But I guess Anna isn't on social media. She could be angry. It's hard to put yourself into somebody else's head when they're so much older than you – and a woman – hmm – I find it hard enough to understand my mum – and she's always telling me to put myself in her place. But Katy said Anna had never told anybody about her adopted son – her family made her so ashamed. Must have been a different world then. I know quite a few single mums – they seem OK. They tell all their friends and their families are good with it. I suggested Peter and Katy talk to Elizabeth first since she's the yes-woman and often speaks for them all. She might know the best way to tell everybody. I'd hate to see the Travel Club break up – they're like my grannies. They even laugh at my jokes. And they feed me.

Elizabeth came first thing, took the magazine, sat down and read it without comment. Katy was worried because the yes-woman was taking so long to work through it, then realised that she was reading again, and again. Not a word came from her mouth, but her face grew paler and paler and tears started to gleam in her eyes. In the space of ten minutes, the lines deepened from her cheeks to her mouth, so she looked ten years older. Justin, who had also been watching over her, made a cup of tea and bent down to put it in her hand. She looked up, gave him a wobbly smile and burst into tears.

Finally, the words staggered out: 'How… could… she!'

Justin put the tea on the magazine table, pulled up a chair next to her and put his arm around her trembling shoulders. He had no words, no suggestions, no jokes, nothing that would fix the situation, but he held her against his young, bony body, absorbing the sobbing and feeling the sorrow.

Peter was watching in amazement at the transformation of his nephew. As the crying subsided, Justin pulled a wad of tissues from the box Katy was holding and offered them. Elizabeth blew her nose, wiped her eyes, and took the cup of tea off the table. As she sipped, she calmed, and then turned to Justin.

'What a lovely boy you are,' she patted his blushing cheek. 'I'm sorry.' She looked around the room. 'It's just…' Elizabeth was trying to think why she had a knife pushing up under her diaphragm, so her eyes leaked so much, 'I think it's just we've all been so close – like sisters.'

Katy smiled at that.

'And now this might destroy our little family.' Elizabeth pulled in a huge, juddering breath.

'We were hoping you might be able to help us prevent that happening.' Peter said, sitting on the other side of her.

Bookended by uncle and nephew, Elizabeth shook her grey curls, 'I'm not sure how. Anna's been so fragile,' She paused and considered, 'although since she's been living with Kathryn, she seems a little stronger.' She took another firmer breath and gathered her wits. 'Maybe she'll be okay.' She pursed her lips. 'Anna needs to know this first since it mostly concerns her private life.' She frowned. 'Can I take the magazine?'

Peter nodded and handed it back to her.

'I'll go and see them this afternoon and we can discuss it. Then I think, if Anna is happy to, we should meet as usual,' Elizabeth said, praying silently: 'Please God let it be all right, but she put on her most positive smile as she waved them all goodbye and slipped out into the stream of shoppers.'

Wow, thought Justin, this is one steely granny.

Katy sent Bob to the cake shop early to buy an array of the Six Sisters' favourite cakes.

Justin was told he was on tea duty and Peter was informed he was to sit and wait at the table, so they had his support from the very start. Katy would deal with any errant customers and she had rescheduled all their other meetings, so the women had their full attention. Peter decided he quite liked being organised like this, although he was unsure of his role.

'Just smile at them,' Katy had assured him, 'and here's three boxes of tissues in case you need them.'

I won't need that many tissues, he thought, I haven't got a cold. Then he realised the tissues weren't for him – oh no, women's tears! He had tried to swap tea duty with Justin, but his nephew wasn't having any of it.

'You can do it,' Katy assured Peter as she pushed him into the chair and planted a reassuring kiss on the top of his blond head.

He was momentarily confused. Did she really do that? Where did that come from? Justin was looking daggers at him. Hmmm – teach him to swap next time, Peter thought, satisfyingly.

Elizabeth, Kathryn, Anna, and Kim all came through the door on time. They sat down, as if it was any other day, and Justin began making the tea and coffee.

Patsy rushed through the door ten minutes later. 'Sorry, sorry,' she apologised, 'I was trying to find a car park.'

Still nothing was mentioned, and Peter produced his lists about the trip and they discussed what they still had to complete. He was also working on their budget, he told them, and wanted a wish list from each of them of what else they would like to do in Europe and he would see what he could manage.

Deep into this discussion, they suddenly noticed Di was sitting among them. Katy had seen her come quietly into the shop and Justin had already got her a cappuccino. The room was struck with a sudden silence.

Di looked amused. 'Before you say any more, I have something to tell you.' She produced a copy of *Travel Europe* from her shopping bag and flourished it in front of their faces. 'I've had an article published about the Travel Club.'

Di paused dramatically.

Lady Macbeth style, Justin thought – on the train he had been catching up on English.

'And they want more,' Di concluded.

Katy looked around the room, trying to find the words to describe the looks on everybody's faces. "Surprised" did not come close. Even "amazed" was too soft. "Astonished" got closer. "Stunned" applied to all of them. "Flabbergasted" was nearer still. "Gobsmacked" seemed literal. And Anna – well, Anna's feelings were staggering across her face like a drunk moving towards the toilet.

'What?' Di laughed. 'You didn't think I could do it?'

Her question robbed nearly everyone of their speech.

Finally, Elizabeth spoke up. 'We didn't think you *would* do it. You've betrayed Anna's confidence.'

'No, no…' Di was back-pedalling fast – it wasn't supposed to go like this. 'You told us all about it,' she said, looking straight at Anna, who looked away.

'Did the magazine ask if you had permission to share personal stories?' Peter asked softly.

'Well… no… not exactly. I told them this was all part of a sales campaign and they were happy to have something from a personal angle – and I changed your names.' She looked around at the now stony faces. 'They like real stories.' Di was faltering

Patsy was totally shocked. 'Don't we all, but you usually ask a person first before you share their business! It's one thing to talk about it here among friends and another to expose them to the whole world.'

'I thought you'd like to see yourselves in print.' Di's voice was truculent now.

'You thought you'd like to see *yourself* in print.' Kathryn' voice was rising as well, shocking them all with her hard-bitten tone.

'Well, if that's how you feel.' Di jumped to her feet.

'Sit down.' Katy came behind her and gently pushed her back into the chair. 'And let's talk about this some more.'

Di looked back over her shoulder at the black fingernails rising back up off her shoulders.

'The way I see it, Anna could sue you if she wanted,' Katy added.

Di opened her mouth to speak but Katy ignored her.

'Or she could forgive you if you promise in future to show her – and everybody else – anything about them you want to publish – before you do it.'

Di considered this.

'And maybe – just maybe – we could get some special deals for the trip from the magazine.' Katy had one more thing to add. 'And maybe, Di could donate some of what she has earned towards the journey.'

Di's eyes narrowed. This was a lot to digest in one bite.

The meeting agreed to think on it and returned to the morning tea Bob had provided. With chocolate cake in their mouths and hot drinks in their bellies, things improved. They began to talk about other things and Di, very wisely, kept her head down.

Phew, thought Peter, that was close. As he bit into the cake, he glanced back at Katy, who was grinning like a little cat.

~ DI ~

I don't really know what to do next. I thought I was giving them such a great gift and instead I upset everybody. Welcome to my life. I just don't seem to get the social stuff. I wouldn't be upset if somebody wrote about me. How come they are?

The sad thing is that before this, for the first time in ages, I felt comfortable. We were always talking about travel – one of my favourite topics – apart from My Kitchen Rules *– and they were all so friendly.*

Katy wants me to contact the editor of the magazine and ask them would they like more – and here's the catch – what they can offer the Travel Club. I don't really mind about the money, what I was really trying to do was get back into publication. So, I guess if I can help their dreams by writing more, then they can help me with my dream.

What I'm most scared of is sharing the text before I publish it. What if they don't like it? I know I'm sensitive, but this sort of writing always feels like I'm ripping out my guts and showing it to people. Well, I guess if I am writing about them, I'm ripping out their guts. So maybe, fair's fair.

'That went well.' Katy said as she sat back down in the abandoned agency.

'It did?' Peter was shoving the tissue boxes back in the cupboard.

'Yes, it did.'

'So how do you describe "well"?' Peter plonked down on the chair next to her and it skidded slightly towards her.

'No blood on the floor.' She smiled at him.

'They're all old ladies.'

'You think that makes a difference?'

'Well, no, but it slows them down a bit. One of them could've offered to go 'round and break Di's kneecaps, I guess.'

'They're the Six Sisters, not the mafia.'

Peter laughed. 'I don't know, I wouldn't want to meet them all together on a dark night.'

'Well, you're going to have to,' she said, and he squinted at her words. 'I mean if you travel with them, it will be dark sometimes. Unless you mean to lock yourself in your room when the sun goes down?'

'Hmm. It's a thought.' He laughed. 'No, I think they're mostly harmless.'

'Just as well,' said Katy and winked at him.

What on earth did that mean, thought Peter.

'And I think Di will be more careful in what she writes next time,' she added.

'It was a great article,' said Peter pursing his lips, 'it'd be a pity to gag her completely.'

'I don't think we will. In fact,' Katy sucked in a deep, slow breath all the way down her diaphragm and Peter tried not to notice her breasts rise, 'we might get lots more good stories because the women feel their memories are valued.'

Wow, he thought, I've employed a psychologist.

'My nanna used to say that women often didn't talk about their lives because they thought they weren't important. She always said history was *his* story,' Katy said sagely.

'You're probably right. But things are changing.' He closed his eyes and leaned precariously back in the chair. 'Let's see what we can wring out of the magazine towards their trip.' He bounced back up and looked her in the eyes. 'That was a brilliant idea.'

Katy batted her eyelashes at him. 'Thank you. I'm always considering new marketing opportunities. It'll get our name out there and we might get work with internet enquiries. Have to employ somebody to look after them then.'

Justin had just shoved the door open after carrying Patsy's shopping to the carpark. 'I could do that.'

Peter's head was shaking with horror. His sister would kill him if he took Justin away from his studies. Mind you, Peter thought as his head steadied, Justin had to be at his studies to be taken away from them.

Di asked Bob to help her with approaching the magazine. His suggestion was that they make an appointment with the editor, just to have a chat about travel generally and where it was heading, so she would know the sorts of articles were publishable. This impressed Di – it would never have occurred to her. She liked to email people.

At the next Travel Club meeting, she was telling them all about how clever Bob was at business. 'Softly, softly,' he'd said. 'Let's see if we can establish a relationship with them and then they might like to come to the party and do something for our lovely ladies.' The Six Sisters sighed collectively at his description. Bob had been sent out for the morning tea, so they felt they could talk about him.

Peter was also out this morning and Katy kept her head down supposedly absorbed in her computer screen.

Justin was downright fascinated. He was transfixed. What an education he got from them – beats school, hands down. He rose to get some paper to take their tea and coffee orders – although his list was merely to please them, they had the same every week.

'Have you noticed Bob is looking more trim?' asked Patsy.

They all nodded. 'And he doesn't feel the need to finish off the morning tea anymore,' added Elizabeth. 'I think he's happier.'

'It's hard to tell, really.' Kim was smiling at Justin as he wrote down her hot chocolate on his list and she nodded her agreement. 'He is so good at saving face.' She thought for a little. 'Although, now I think he says what he thinks.'

The white stripe in Di's dark hair was bouncing up and down. 'He certainly told me what he thought about what I'd done. But once he said it, there were no more recriminations, just a business-like "don't do it again" and then we were working out what to do next.' She smiled as sweetly as they had ever seen. 'It feels good to have somebody like that to work with.'

Anna's eyebrows rose slowly – like the Van Gogh poster of a cantilever bridge, Elizabeth thought, but she said nothing. Di needed a keeper, she was thinking, and Bob needed somebody to keep. Strange bedfellows but somehow suitable – Elizabeth almost laughed. You never know, really.

She would have been fascinated to know that Katy was thinking the same thing – in her rather more modern fashion.

Because Peter was out, they decided to discuss the Travel Club's future appointments with Katy. These were coming in thick and fast now because people had read the magazine. Would these convert to bookings? Katy couldn't answer that, but she was trying to ensure that she only called the women in when it was genuine and not just snooping.

A week later, Katy was contacted by the publicity department of a travel company that ran cruises through Europe. The woman asked a lot of questions about the Travel Club and Katy had trouble trying to work out appropriate responses. 'Let me get our public relations man to give you a ring,' she eventually answered, when she could get a word in, 'he's out of the office.' Well, he didn't actually come into the office today, she was thinking, but, on the surface, it was true. 'I'll give him your name and number.'

Peter walked in just as she finished off the call. 'For me?'

She shook her head. 'I don't think so. I think we should get Bob to handle it. They want to know about our Travel Club.'

Tricky, thought Peter. 'I think Bob's just the man.'

'Can I call him on his days off?'

'He'd be upset if you didn't.' Peter laughed. 'He half-lives here, anyway.'

In fact, Bob was beside himself when he got the call. He ran around the room like a triumphant soccer fan in his y-fronts with his T-shirt over his head – the Travel Club would have been shocked to see this – shouting, 'yes, yes, yes!' Until, the old man in the flat next door banged on the wall.

He and Di had been to see the editor and discussed a range of things. He'd gradually led the exchange to what perks the various advertisers might be able to offer the Travel Club in exchange for their stories. Obviously, the magazine people had been talking to their clients. So, he rang the woman from the cruise company back and offered to come in for a meeting. 'Face to face is the way to go,' he'd told Di – a thing that she found difficult. 'All these emails and even phone conversations are open to various interpretations – and can be ignored – but face to face, you develop a relationship.'

And so, it was that the following week, Bob came with his best suit, having already purchased the morning tea, and informed the Travel Club that he was expecting a visitor – with a proposal – about which they would have to make a decision. He said these three words as if they were chocolate coated, savouring them, rolling them around in his mouth and handing them on like precious gems.

'How,' he said with a dramatic flourish that would have left Katy's nanna gasping, 'would you all like to cruise down the Rhine?' He looked around the table like a magician pulling a white elephant from his good suit pocket.

Not much silenced the Six Sisters. With a collective longevity approaching half a millennium, they had seen and heard most of what the world offered or downright forced down their throats. But, in their whole long lives, very rarely had they got anything without working for it. Suspicion crowded into the room. Eyes narrowed. Breaths hissed in. Lips thinned. Scepticism's scent slid through the room spreading like bubonic plague from one to the next.

'And what,' Katy had risen to her black-booted feet, 'do guests have to do to travel like that?'

The mind boggled, thought Peter, and then dismissed any errant boggling – they were too old for that. A swivel of heads turned first to Katy, then back to Bob. Like watching Wimbledon, Peter thought.

'Talk,' said Bob. 'Just talk.' He could feel his gut burning all the way down and he'd forgotten to bring his heartburn medication.

There was a long silence while the room digested his proposal.

'Oh,' said Anna finally, and the heads turned to her, 'that's easy. We can do that. We've had so much practice. We're used to eating for our words.' And suddenly, the room was filled with honey light and acceptance and joy.

'We do love to talk,' said Kim, shyly, 'and maybe I can get my husband to come now that it is so cheap.'

When Camilla from the cruise company came, they welcomed her like a long-lost daughter, regaled her with various and hilarious stories about their travels and the Travel Club, and allowed Bob to do all the negotiating on their parts. As she left, she shook hands with everybody and lastly, Peter.

'Remarkable, remarkable,' she was saying and shaking her head in disbelief as she tried to understand the source of all her inner joy.

'Yes, they are,' said Peter. 'Quite remarkable.'

~ KATY ~

My list, in no particular order – although, of course it will need to be in order to know what needs to be done first…

1. *Get six older women (Nanna said never call women old or even elderly), one elderly man and one hot, yummy man across the world – delete hot and yummy – he can't see that – how did that get there?*
2. *Ask cruise company for available dates*
3. *Work out who is going to share with who (should that be whom?) on the cruise*

4. *Organise Anna to meet her son*
5. *Talk to the cruise company about having Anna's son on board if he wants to come*
6. *Ask whether Anna's son would like to go on the cruise and share a room with Peter. (That would be safer, I don't really trust Di with Peter – even if she and Bob do have a thing going on.)*
7. *Ask Kim if she would like them to visit London so she could have time with her daughter.*
8. *Check all the passports to make sure they will be valid. Including Peter's. Remember you can't use them in the last six months before they expire. Hope nobody expires on the trip.*
9. *Work out where else the club would like to go*
10. *Organise tickets home again*
11. *Make up another list of things to take with them*
12. *Book Bob to work full time while they are away*

My Secret List…

13. *Look on Passport to see how old Peter is*
14. *Ask Justin to work weekends and as much as possible if it is school holidays*
15. *Ask Justin does Peter have a girlfriend – or if he ever had one, and what she was like.*
16. *Tell Justin not to tell Peter she had been asking.*
17. *Grow hair and see what colour it is.*
18. *Buy some new shoes – maybe heels – like Camilla wore – and red lipstick*

'I have a list,' said Katy on the following Saturday morning, waving it under Peter's nose. She had decided to print it, so it looked more formal, although, to be honest, she wanted his input into it. 'I'll need your passport,' she said eyes sliding away, 'and everybody else's of course.'

Peter's smile lit up his face, he had decided he quite liked being organised, 'Wow, the 12 Commandments.'

'There were only 10 Commandments, you're thinking of the apostles.'

He was momentarily side-tracked. 'I'm sure there were a dozen. I remember my mum saying the eleventh one was something about not being found out.' He winked at Katy.

Better hide the rest of that list, she was thinking. Oh no, did she leave the comments about him being hot and yummy on the page? She glanced at the document on the computer, phew – no – it had been edited down to the bare bones.

'So, what do you think?' she repeated.

'Hmm. I think… I think… it is a very good list and… I am hoping you will make me some more lists to take with me on the trip.'

Katy glowed like a neon light. 'Certainly, sir,' in her official phone voice. 'How many would you like?'

Transfixed by her offer, Peter gazed into Katy's face. There was something different, and he liked it. He wanted to sniff to see if it was a different perfume, but realised she might think that was weird, and the last thing he wanted her to think of him was that he had a cold. Let's see – still has the Fire Truck hair. And the piercings are all there, maybe a little more ornate. Eye makeup – yep – maybe not so dark today. And then he got to her lips. Bright red to match her tresses – yes, he thought tresses. Wow. He'd only ever seen her with black or maybe purple lips. The bright red outlined the shape of her mouth and increased the puffy softness of the pucker. The store's lights slid like bright sun rays between them. Like a fridge magnet to a stainless-steel sink, he could feel his lips moving towards hers, the beat of his heart weaving erratically.

Just then, Justin came through the door like a green P Plate driver. 'Hey, hey, *hey*,' he said as he unplugged his headphone from one ear. 'What's up?'

The light shattered, and a million sparking tears of disappointment speared downwards in Peter's belly. Peter found himself gasping and grabbing the nearest magazine, shoving it in Justin's face and saying, 'How about you do some research for us today.' He ripped the book open and poked his finger at the first page he found. 'Look around for some good things to do there.'

'I thought you didn't do trips to the Middle East,' Justin said, eyes wide. He glanced slightly sideways and noticed Katy's back firmly turned to them, shaking slightly.

'You never know. Good to be prepared. Learnt that as a Scout. Always be prepared.' Peter's words were coming out in gasps.

'Prepared for what?' Justin asked.

'Anything,' said Peter, trying to breathe deeply before he spoke, 'anything at all.'

Wow, thought Justin, he's losing it. Just like Mum and Dad.

'Spend an hour on this and give me some options, and then we might sit down and talk about tourism for your age group.'

'Really?' Justin was impressed. Nobody had mentioned his travelling.

'Yep. Cradle to Grave – that's us. Always ready for anything.' Peter smiled in what he thought might be an avuncular fashion. Except that he was not ready for anything. Not ready for those scarlet lips that were beckoning across the room. Not ready to start dating again. Not ready to try to work out what a woman wanted – or needed – or even meant when she said stuff. That's one thing he never did a scout badge for – girlfriends.

'How soon do you think they could be ready to travel?' Katy asked Peter on Monday morning.

He was stripping off his coat. Autumn was tentatively tiptoeing in, scattering rusty leaves outside the mall. The long Indian summer seemed to be withdrawing into its tepee.

'From my end, any time. Everybody has their passports now and we have a fair amount in the special fund. We just need to check their availability.'

He looked at her with his head on one side – very attractive, Katy's nanna inner voice was saying – with big eyes like a cocker spaniel.

'Why?' he asked.

She was smiling at her own thoughts, controlling her amusement. 'Just got an email from Camilla and they're offering a European River Trip, if we can make the air fares. They would also like the Travel Club to have some small get-togethers with the other passengers on board, so the ladies could work their magic.'

'Let's put it to them. We can research fare prices and see what we can come up with,' he said. 'I think they've been ready for quite some time.' Peter had decided the professional approach was the way to speak to her, Katy noted with some amusement.

'Camilla has asked if Anna's son would like to come on the trip with them.' She glanced down. 'And if you could share a room with him.' She didn't add that this had been her suggestion. 'Would that be okay with you?'

Peter had to reorganise his concept of the trip in his brain. He'd imagined the cabin on the vessel as his private retreat, he didn't really mind how big or where it was, just a place to go and hide when the questions and conversations threatened to engulf him. Somewhere he could get the sports results. He sighed – dramatically, Katy thought.

'Will he be on the same deal?' he asked.

Katy nodded and shut her eyes waiting for his answer.

'I guess I'll manage,' Peter said.

Katy's eyes sprang open and her smile lit up her face, settled in her beautiful green eyes and crackled through the air between them.

Manage *who*, Peter wondered, as the excitement rocketed down his body.

CHAPTER EIGHT

~ PETER ~

June, July, August and then we're off to Europe. Twelve weeks and Peter Piper and his travelling circus hit the road. Well, not the road exactly, more like the sky and hit is not a word I care to use about flying.

I can see myself sitting at the airport like Rincewind, checking out the nearest exits. It seemed like such a great idea. Was I railroaded into this? Skyroaded, really. I think it was my idea – or Katy's. Does that mean I think Katy's responsible – and for what?

And there's another thing. I'm finding it hard to breathe when Katy is around. Heart beating faster, and I can't think about what down-below's considering – that does lead to disaster. She's nearly ten years younger than me. I wonder if that matters? The little man in my brain – and other places – is screaming at me that I only have twelve weeks to work this out.

The thing is – I've really come to like and appreciate her. No – I will not say love – but every minute with her is like sitting on a glass stove top. I want to move away because I know I'm going to get burned – but I enjoy the heat.

I need a plan. Of course, I pay her to do the planning. This is how it goes – she plans – I execute – we're all happy. So, she is responsible.

I remember that joke – a man's gotta have a secretary, he can't blame everything on the government. Hang on, I think it should be a man's gotta have a wife. Uh-oh…

On Saturday afternoon, Justin came through the door like a

toddler on the run. Peter glanced down the mall to see if Carol was following. Nope, all clear. Why did Justin look so pleased with himself – and why did he have a full backpack over his shoulder? Was he running away from home?

'What are you doing here?' Peter asked shortly.

'I thought I'd come and help.'

'My agreement with your mother was once a fortnight. You came last week.' Peter was trying to be firm.

'I got a text from Kim's son asking me to lunch with all of you tomorrow,' Justin said. Peter was trying to work out how Kim's son would have Justin's mobile number and barely heard the rest of what Justin said, 'and I told mum you'd invited me to stay over tonight and go with you.'

The words sank in and Peter gaped at his nephew's audacity.

Katy was snorting quietly to herself in the corner.

'Why would you do that?' Peter was struggling with the concept of bald-faced falsehood.

'I thought we could watch the footie on TV together. That's what you're going to do, isn't it? Pizza and footie on Saturday night?'

Peter didn't really want to discuss his lack of private life in front of Katy. 'Don't you have something better to do?' Peter went on, 'I hear people your age party on Saturday nights?'

'Some might.'

'So, what do you do?'

Justin looked past him, out the door. 'The oldies usually go out and I keep the Xbox warm.' That was his mother's favourite expression. So far, he'd avoided the big snip to the power plug.

'Well, I might have other plans,' Peter huffed.

'No way.' Justin laughed. 'You never have other plans. Mum calls you the man without a plan. So, I thought I'd make one for you.'

Katy's snorts were getting louder and louder, Peter felt like telling her to blow her nose.

'And,' added Justin, 'I thought maybe first we could go to the pub and have a drink after work.'

'You're underage,' Peter said, knowing his sister would have apoplexy, 'you don't drink.' And mentally added that this was probably untrue.

'I drink coke.' Justin had him there. 'How about the three of us go down the pub tonight and I'll have a coke, thanks.'

'What a good idea,' Katy's voice was shaking, 'just the three of us.'

Peter looked sideways at her and caught the ghost of a wink. Hmmm, he thought – three was too big a number for him.

~ KATY ~

It was so good to have lunch at Kim's place. We had great discussions about the holiday. And the best thing was her husband decided to go on the trip with her. Just fixed it with the tour company – phew. That left Di on her own, but she reluctantly agreed to have a single cabin.

With eleven weeks until departure, there was a lot they wanted to know. It was like being back at school – but I was the teacher. Just as well the QM had a notepad in her bag and lent it to me. Clothes, shoes, suitcases, weather, food, toilets, flu shots – nothing was left unplanned. Dad said it was better than watching the footie, seeing me field so many questions. Wow! And, I suspect, it surprised him that his daughter had all the answers.

He had asked me where I was going on Sunday and I told him a client's home for lunch.

Up went his eyebrows. 'Didn't know clients entertained agents.'

'Special clients,' I replied.

'Ah, the Six Sisters,' he said knowingly.

'Do you want to come?'

'Me – why would I come?'

'Kim said I could bring somebody.'

'Who's Kim?'

'The lady whose house we're going to. But I thought you'd want to watch the footie.' I didn't tell him Kim probably meant a boyfriend.

'Humph. It's a bye, they're not playing.'

'Why don't you come then?'

'All right, I will. With your cooking, a fella needs a good feed occasionally.' I was still staring at him as he began to grin.

Kim had *asked me did I want to bring somebody. She's the least nosy of the Six Sisters but they're all very keen to know about our love lives. They even ask Justin how his love life is going. Teenage boys blush so well. So, I decided to tease her and said I'd see what I could do. At the time I was completely without plans. But dad really needs to get out and talk to other people more and the Six Sisters are around his age – so I took him along.*

Talk about causing a stir! Peter nearly exploded when I walked in and said I brought the man I lived with. Dad let me down badly. 'I don't live with you – you live with me,' he said, 'it's my unit. Kids these days! What d'you do with them?' When I said he was my dad, we all had a good laugh. And then Peter walked straight up to him, shook him by the hand and told him how lovely it was to meet him. What a man!

'Do you think they're all happy with the travel plans?' Peter stopped staring at his computer and glanced out of the corner of his eyes at Katy as he spoke.

'I hope so.' She was never really sure how to take him these days. Was there some part of the plan that was worrying him? 'Did you see anybody looking unhappy?'

'No, not really – except for Di, maybe.'

'Huh. She took off her happy pants weeks ago – except when Bob's around.'

Peter's mouth gaped under his rounded eyes. 'Really?'

Katy flicked her eyebrows up enticingly and her pussycat grin returned, pinning him to the chair. 'Really. Haven't you noticed?'

He wanted to say, of course I have, but then thought – why lie?

'Nope. Not at all.' Then he wondered what else he was missing

'Well, now you can watch them too. It's fun.'

'Other people watch them?'

Katy slid across on her wheelie chair and bumped into his to break her journey. 'Justin was the first one to point it out to me.'

'Justin!'

'Justin. He's becoming quite the emo-meter – all that training from the Six Sisters.'

'You can get training in it?'

'Of course, you can. It's all in the facial expressions and body language. Kathryn pointed it out to Justin – it's *all* in the body language.' She patted him firmly on the knee. 'He told the sisters he has been practising it on his parents.'

Peter was so distracted by the warm feel of her hand on his leg, sending messages upwards, that he almost missed the rest of what she had to say.

'His parents!' he cried, horror-struck.

'And his school teachers. He says he's getting on much better with them now that he can read their bodies.'

What have I done, thought Peter, which was closely followed by what Katy's body language was saying. He would have to get some lessons too. What was *his* body language doing? As he reached out and took that hot little hand in his, his subconscious spewed straight out of his mouth: 'How about coming to the pub for a drink after work?' She nodded and his conscience gained control of his frontal lobe and added, 'We can talk about the trip.'

~ KIM ~

Ten weeks and we will be flying away. I can't believe Tam is coming. We are going to end in London and stay on with our daughter for two more weeks. He finally agreed after the Travel Club came for Sunday lunch. My son and his wife

cooked for us – all our special dishes – and we had a lovely time.

Tam was slow to start, he is a quiet man, and they are all strangers to him, but he invited Peter to sit next to him and asked him very gently about the agency, and travel, and his life. And Peter, who is also a quiet man, began to share his story: what he had done before owning the travel agency, his travels, and then coming home to care for his mother.

As they spoke the other conversations quietened and I could see we were all listening to Peter and hearing things we had never heard before – and never imagined. It's funny – you look at a person and you only ever see them in the place you know them. Opposite me, I could see Katy's eyes filling up with tears as Peter talked about juggling work with being a carer, and then having to be home permanently as his mother reached her last days. And about how the agency had given him something new to do in the darkness that followed – and then the arrival of the Travel Club.

Now Tam can see why these people are family to me. My son and his wife are amazed that we're both going, but happy for us too. And I think they're entrusting us to Peter who will care for all of us – as he did for his mother.

'Thank you so much for the lovely lunch,' said Elizabeth, ever the yes-woman, used to speaking for all of them. The others nodded in agreement.

Peter had stopped thinking of them as pigeons, but the co-ordination of heads brought to mind the first time he had spoken to them and he smiled at his computer at the warmth of memory.

'You're very welcome.' Kim was delighted. She had enjoyed the day so much, showing her family another side of her had been so satisfying, it had made her feel young again – and interesting – and whole.

'It won't be long, and we'll be eating together regularly,' Kathryn said and then looked sideways, 'Sorry, Katy and Bob, I didn't mean to leave you out.'

'No problem,' replied Bob, 'somebody has to hold the fort, eh

Katy?'

Katy nodded briefly and glanced over the heads of the women and out into the mall beyond. Peter noticed her eyes glisten as she glanced away – wow his observation was improving – perhaps she was a bit sad to be left at home. She'd never said anything. But then, he didn't ask. They'd been to the pub for a drink a couple of times last week and this week he planned to ask her out for a meal. He'd decided she was bright and funny and also very wise. What his body was saying was that she was also cute and warm and quite delicious – and would be a perfect fit in his arms. But, he decided, while they were in the office he would concentrate on her intellectual side.

Getting a grip on his thoughts, Peter turned to Kim, 'I really enjoyed talking to your husband. And I'm delighted to hear that he is going to join us.'

'So am I,' said Kim, 'and quite surprised, even though I *had* asked him before. He's still a bit worried about leaving Australia but it will be okay with you taking us.'

'That's why we're going,' said Anna to Peter, 'because we trust you.'

And this time the brightness in Katy's eyes spilled over and trickled down her cheeks,

Down, down, down he drifted, where dead dreams come alive again.

~ BOB ~

Last night my daughter rang me and asked me how I was.

'Fine,' I said, 'how are you going? And my grandson?'

'Good, good,' she said. 'I was wondering if you'd like to spend some time with him?'

I was so excited. I see them rarely. I have never been asked to look after him before and he is nearly twelve months old.

'Well,' she said, 'the thing is,' there was a pause while she organised her words, 'I'm going back to work in a couple of months and I wondered if you'd look after him.'

'What, full time?' My brain was racing.

'Well, I asked Mum but she says she's too busy and so I thought you had nothing to do and you might like to.'

All this time, I thought, all this time, and now she asks me when I have a job.

'I'm sorry darling, but I work two days a week at present and in nine weeks' time I have a contract for three weeks of full time work. I really cannot afford to turn it down.'

There was blank silence on the other end of the phone then she said, 'Oh well, never mind. I'll see you some time,' and hung up.

I was asking myself, is this all I am good for? Should I turn down any opportunity to be with my grandson? I was torn in two. I rang my daughter back.

'I'm sorry,' I said.

'No, no, Dad, I'm sorry,' she replied, 'I'm sorry. I was ready to use you just like all the women in your life. I'm ashamed of myself.' She was crying.

'No, no,' I said, 'I want to be used.'

'Yeah, but not used and abused. I know how hard things have been for you. I'm glad you have work now. I'll figure this out. Maybe, when you finish working full time, you could do a bit of babysitting.' I heard the hope in her voice — and forgiveness. We could be father and daughter — and grandson again.

'I'd like to. Let me know how you go and we'll see what we can work out,' I replied.

I hung up.
And sobbed.
And sobbed.
And sobbed.

School bag hanging off his shoulder and phone in hand, Justin came through the door like a dog on a dodgem. 'Hey, hey. What's happening?'

Bob was alone in the agency, tidying the magazines in his last clean of the day. He shook his head at Justin. 'What are you doing here?'

'Pete said I could come and watch the Wallabies play with him. You know, uncle nephew bonding over pizza and footie.'

Bob nodded.

'Are you okay?'

'Sure. Just family stuff.'

'C'mon. You can tell me. I tell you all about my fights with Mum and Dad.'

Bob smiled at that. He was always emotionally caught between this dear boy and the angst he caused for his parents. Bob found this a bit hard to understand. His son and daughter had grown up self-motivated and he and their mother had left them to decide for themselves what they wanted to do in life. Of course, technology was not the force then that it was now.

They sat down in the Travel Club corner. 'My daughter asked me to look after my grandson,' said Bob.

'Sounds like fun,' Justin said.

'At the same time, I'm working here.'

'Oh.' Justin was beginning to get the gist of the problem. 'Well, you can't. You promised the Travel Club you'd look after everything here.'

'Yes, I did. And no. I can't, can I?'

'I mean, you couldn't bring him in to work.' Justin was labouring through the issue.

Bob shook his head.

'Although the Six Sisters would love him.'

Bob smiled.

'So maybe,' added Justin, 'when they come home again you could bring him sometimes and, in between, your daughter could find another place for him. Couldn't she leave it for a bit before she goes back to work?'

Bob put his hand on Justin's shoulder. 'Thanks mate. I'll talk to her some more about it. It's just so hard because you always want to do your best for your kids.'

Justin nodded and wondered if that's what his parents were doing – their best – and he was not appreciating it at all. Hmm, something to think about.

~ KATHRYN ~

So much to do in eight weeks. Just as well retirement's been on my mind. I've been encouraging all my students above 8th grade to start teaching beginners and small grades themselves; showing them how to go about it and have them sitting in on lessons and even contributing. Now I'm simply going to hand my pupils over to these student teachers for a month. More perplexing was what to do with those senior pupils. However, I've a good friend who is also a music teacher and she has offered to have them while I am away. I'm leaving them all in good hands.

How exciting it will be to be in Vienna. Anna and I are going back there to spend two weeks at the end of the cruise. I cannot – CANNOT – wait to hear the music of Strauss in his own city. And – AND – we are going to Saltzburg as part of the cruise. Everybody else at Kim's luncheon was talking about the Sound of Music – a bit of wine and we can imagine ourselves in those hills alive with the sound of music. Patsy even sang "Climb Every Mountain" in a couple of keys – mostly – that quelled the musical outpourings. Lovely, lovely – but I want to walk the halls of Mozart's house. I cannot wait. Still there is so much to do. Just as well I like planning.

'Do you think he'll like me?' Anna asked Kathryn as they sipped their breakfast tea. They were sitting in Anna's chairs at Anna's table in the breakfast room, and the contrast to her landlady's belongings was tearing her heartstrings. Who was she, she thought, to claim motherhood to this wonderful man?

'Of course, he will,' Kathryn answered.

Anna shook her head. 'I've been watching that show on TV where people find their families. Sometimes people don't get on.'

'*He* wrote to *you*, didn't he?'

Anna nodded. 'Yes but…' She stopped, searching for the right words.

Kathryn waited, watching her friend carefully, letting her work through the process.

Finally, Anna lifted her head. 'I am nothing, a nobody, an old woman alone. He is an engineer, a wealthy man with a family and friends.'

'You have friends,' Kathryn assured her, taking both Anna's hands in hers, 'and you have family – and they are waiting for you.'

Anna gripped Kathryn's hands tightly, pulling strength from her friend's words and spirit. She took a deep breath, pushing down her fears. 'Yes…. Yes, I have.'

~ ANNA ~

I cannot believe this is happening. In seven weeks, I will be holding my son in my arms. It is a day I never dreamed would come. But I'm returning to the place of so much pleasure and so much pain. At least my friends will be with me. Kathryn is always so firm – like a strong framework holding me up – allowing me to turn to the future. So much to do. Should I leave my hair grey? Kathryn thinks so – but get it styled she said. We're going to her hairdresser – the one at the mall that serves coffee and cake and advice for nothing extra. Having a double appointment. Then, Kathryn said – THEN we are going shopping for clothes. By the time we get to Europe, it will be northern autumn. Perfect time for some new holiday outfits. It's nice to have somebody care about what I wear. I'm learning to care again.

'How are you going on that list?' Bob asked Peter.

'Which one?' Peter replied.

Katy was out at lunch and Bob had called in, supposedly to check up on arrangements. Well that's what he had said, truth be told he liked being in the agency, paid or unpaid. He looked cagey, 'Any of them?' Then thought again, 'How many do you have?'

Peter shook his head, 'Too many. She's gone list crazy,' gesturing towards Katy's empty chair with his head, 'or maybe she just thinks I need them to keep up.'

Bob wasn't sure what to say. He knew Peter could be disorganised and, personally, he loved a list – it helped him through the day.

'There's the itinerary with everybody's bookings,' Peter picked up a huge folder of papers and slapped it down on the desktop. 'Then there's all the women's next of kin, medication and even funeral arrangements.' He rolled his eyes like he was disapproving but really it scared the socks off him. 'A packing list for the women – I hope I don't have to check their bags,' he added as an afterthought. His voice was getting louder and louder as the pile climbed. 'A list of possible places to go when we get free time. FREE TIME – that's a joke.' He shuffled through the rest of the papers, 'And somewhere in all these chopped-down trees there's a list of what the travel company wants us to talk about.' He gave up, stood up, and with a wide, backhanded swing, swept all the papers onto the floor. 'I quit,' he declared.

The glass door shushed open with a cloud of exotic perfume and Katy came in. 'What's all this?' she said, picking her way through the papers and stopping directly in front of Peter.

Fascinating, thought Bob, as Peter gazed at her.

'I quit,' Peter reiterated.

'You can't quit, you're the boss.'

'I can quit if I want to.'

A little boy voice, Katy thought. 'But you don't really want to.' She pushed him gently into his chair, bent over in front of him in her short skirt and picked up the papers, tidying them with a deft clunk on the table top, and placing them neatly on her desk. 'You're just a bit scared – but it will be okay.'

Mesmerised, thought Bob, Peter was mesmerised like a cat with a cobra.

She was perched on the desk in front of Peter with her hands on his shoulders. 'You know I will organise it all and you just have to follow the instructions – and it *will* work.'

Peter was nodding, his face a grinning mask.

'All this is just in case,' she pointed to the pile of papers, 'but you won't need them.'

Peter nodded again. Then a huge breath came from the bottom of his lungs out his frozen lips, as his face relaxed and he felt the tension drain out of his body.

Katy turned and picked up another piece of paper off her desk. 'But you *will* need this.' She handed it to him. It said: - *PETER'S MASTER LIST.*

The aforementioned groaned.

'It's okay,' she winked, 'this one will fit in your pocket.'

~ ELIZABETH ~

Dear God, help me. Six weeks' time and I am going to be living with Patsy. It was at the lunch at Kim's place that we sorted out who would share with who. Patsy chose me rather than Di – who looked a bit miffed. I offered to have the single cabin – but Di said 'no, no you two go together, I'll be FINE.' And I was too scared to say anything else.

Not sure how I'll cope. Patsy's just so… so… so… and I am not so much. A bit buttoned up, me. If she starts talking about her sex life with Ray, I'm frightened I might burst out and return the favour. Oooh, that would be so bad – makes me feel very wicked. I feel like saying – we all made love – some of us just didn't talk about it. But that would be cruel, and I know it would make her feel wretched. She seems to be trying to find who she was before Ray became so ill and she could feel her life slipping down. Intimacy is certainly high on her list of reminiscences – as if she could summon him through her memories of being one. Maybe we can discuss this obsession.

Dear God, you joined John and me into one person and we were still making love right up until the day he died. The pleasure and the pain of remembering how we enjoyed each other that final morning haunts me. I'm sorry. I made his heart stop – forever. I can't think about that now. It's like a knife splitting me in two. I need to think about something else. I know Patsy never had children. I try not to show her family photos because it must be very distressing for her. There's nobody to say – we'll miss you Mum or Nanna. Or even – can you bring me back whatever? My four are delighted I'm taking a holiday – please, God, look after them all while I'm away.

My eldest daughter is taking my darling dog, Molly, to her place for a bit of "R and R" she says – and maybe some fitness exercises to get rid of the middle age spread. Poor Molly – she does love her snacks. She'll be a new dog by the time I get back – for a month or so, anyway. My friends at church are all wishing me well. Glad to see the back of my sad face. They miss John too – I see them cringe when I say his name.

Please, just let me enjoy the time away.

'Camilla wants to know how often the sisters can have their little tête-à-têtes?' Katy did a great impression of her lipstick model as Peter hunched back to the office.

He had been out looking for some new clothes to take and was totally fed up. It was a mistake to ambush him like that, Katy realised, when it registered that he had not one shopping bag. To hit him with a planning issue after doing something he found so depressing.

'No luck then?' she added, changing tack.

He shook his head. 'I don't know what to buy. Usually, I just find something comfortable, and buy four different colours of the same thing.'

That explained it, thought Katy, she had noticed his matching shirts but thought it was his idea of a uniform. How long had he been doing that, she wondered, the I'll-have-four-of-the-same approach? Probably since his mother stopped buying his clothes. There was something very appealing about a helpless man, she decided, just crying out to be organised. It made her feel all gooey inside – she'd have to take him shopping. She smiled understandingly at him. 'Why don't we ask the sisters what they think about the talk program. My thought would be an hour or so every day, or couple of days, depending on what else was happening, and how they were feeling.'

'They're not young,' said Peter

'But they do love to talk.'

'That's true. And it wouldn't have to be all of them every time.'

'Perhaps we could ask them what topics they'd like to talk about. About travel, I mean.' Katy laughed, and Peter looked at her. 'I mean, if you open it up, Patsy would just talk about her love life.'

Peter was laughing now. 'Let's not get Patsy reminiscing about sex.'

'You never know, it could be very educational,' said Katy, turning away, her shoulders shaking.

Peter's belly summersaulted. Maybe we should get her to teach me, he wanted to say – but didn't.

~ PATSY ~

Darling Ray, I'm off on an adventure in just five weeks, and I've agreed to share a cabin with Elizabeth. Now that will be an adventure. She must be one of the kindest people I know, but sometimes she looks at me like I'm an alien. I've never told her that I grew up in the church. I left because – well, I don't really know why I left – nothing bad happened. I just sort of drifted away – and you rescued me from drowning.

Funny, you always said I rescued you. All those mates you hung out with at the pub. I remember you telling me most of them got smashed and spent their wages on a Friday night and you'd been to quite a few funerals when they died in drunken car accidents. You said, when I came into the pub that night with my girlfriends, you looked at my flowery dress and thought I was a blossom – you often called me that – that I was like a magnet pulling you across the room away from all the mate-ship and jokes and alcohol, and into my world. We didn't need drink to be intoxicated. Love at first sight, you said, or was it the birds and the bees? Both, I think now – and I'm glad it was. It got us through the tough times – and there were enough of those, particularly when the only fertility we had was in our garden. But we clung together on our joint life raft and found peaceful shores at last in just being ourselves.

My darling, I've hungered for those times again – relived them – reworked them – dug down deep into my memories and written them out on pages and pages – explicitly – like a mistress of erotica. I've read them so often they're like living dreams burned into my soul. And finally, my head is starting to clear. You'll always be my heart and soul and I'll love you till all the stars are lost, but to keep on existing, I must find a distant shore where you are not.

I've been talking to God again lately – dare I say, praying – I know you'd be surprised. So maybe, sharing with Elizabeth is just what I need. Some good frank discussion about widowhood (I hate that word) and what comes after.

Winter had ushered in freezing rain, slanting down outside the mall, driving shoppers to brandish their brollies into the fiery flash of air conditioning, and forcing the Travel Club to fear what awaited them in Europe.

'Layers,' pronounced Patsy, 'we'll need layers.'

Anna reflected that she had worn layers when she first emigrated – everything she owned sometimes, layer upon layer just to keep warm. She was damned – yes, damned – if she was going to meet her son dressed as a refugee.

'That's right,' agreed Kathryn, with Anna looking at her horrified, 'something cool first, a warmer top over and then a wind-proof jacket. And comfortable shoes.'

The thought of comfy shoes just made Anna more depressed. It was years since she'd worn heels. When you cleaned people's houses, flatties made your feet last all day – and half the night, sometimes. She wanted her son to be proud of her. Longed for him to see her as a person of value, worthy of having him. All those years of not caring about her appearance and now her stomach churned at the thought of looking like an old woman.

'We'll help you.' Patsy touched Anna on the arm making her jump. 'In fact, we'll all help each other. We could have a packing party at my place.'

'What, take all our clothes to your place?!' Elizabeth was feeling panicky now, she didn't want people going through her clothes.

'If you like,' said Patsy, a little uncertain, 'but why don't we make a list and then we can pull them out and see what we have?' She turned to Elizabeth. 'Then if anybody needs help, they can ask for it.'

Kathryn and Anna were nodding, and Elizabeth's head was moving side to side as if she didn't want to agree, but could see the sense in it.

Katy came over. 'I think that would be great. Let's work on a list.' And she sat down with the women.

Half an hour later, Peter came back into the room and looked at them all writing. 'Is this a list for me?' he smiled, picking up Patsy's list.

'If you like,' said Katy.

'Four pairs of panty hose,' quoted Patsy.

All the colour ran out of Peter's face down to his freezing toes.

'Maybe not,' said Katy to the laughing sisters and took the list off him, giving it back to Patsy. 'It's okay,' she said to Peter, 'I'll write you a packing list – and leave off the panty hose.'

~ JUSTIN ~

How cool is it that I have organised work experience at the Travel Agency again? Four weeks to go and I can work at the agency for three weeks. Dad's not impressed. He wanted me to go to his mate's solicitor's office. But for once, Mum took my side. Maybe tidying up my room helped. You never know – I really cannot work her out. I think she is more of a realist than dad. Either that or the talk we had with the Career Counsellor at school kicked in. I wish it had kicked dad. As if I will ever get the marks to get into law. As if I want to be a solicitor. I really want to study travel, but I don't know how to tell them.

I spend my Saturdays here now and a couple of times I've stayed over with Uncle Pete and then we did something on Sunday. Like the day we went to Kim and Tam's for lunch. The food was absolutely amazing. I mean, you go to Vietnamese restaurants and the food is cool, but this was spectacular. And they kept making me eat more. I had such a good time and they were all old people. Well, older than me – but they treated me like one of them. And Katy brought her dad, so we could talk about the footie – well, that's what she told me. He even asked me if I wanted to go to the footie with him one day. And I might just do that. I could stay at Uncle Pete's house again.

'Show me what you bought,' said Katy to Anna and Kathryn as the Travel Club, sitting knee deep in shopping bags, was sipping their hot drinks. Some of them had come from the dress shop next door where the assistants had fussed over them.

Anna looked sideways at Katy. Surely this exotic young woman couldn't be interested in her? Kathryn was fishing into one of her own bags. Evidently, she was happy for show and tell. Out came three pastel lacy tops and a raspberry weatherproof jacket. Kathryn held them up for approval. Everybody around the table was smiling. How lovely they were, how they'd be perfect for the casual holiday on a riverboat, how they'd suit Kathryn. 'And they were 50% off.' She showed them the tags. 'Show them what you bought Anna.'

Anna shyly pulled her bag up onto the table and started taking out the clothes one by one. Hers were deeper colours with lots of purple and mauve and some bright splashes here and there.

'These are just right for you – so pretty,' said Kim. 'Just like Patsy's garden.'

'And she bought some skirts and pants, too.' Kathryn lifted another of Anna's bags, holding it open as if it could swallow somebody. Everybody leant towards the gaping attraction of new clothes.

'This goes with that,' sang Patsy, as she plucked out bottoms and matched them with tops.

'It's good that they give you so much discount,' said Di, 'but I always think they make them dearer first.'

Anna's face fell, and the rest of the group rushed in to say how much they liked this outfit or that.

Elizabeth was gesturing in the direction of the dress shop next door. 'Next door wants some pictures of us in their outfits on the holiday. They asked us could they blow up our photos and display them on their walls. Can you pass some on to them?' she asked Di.

Anna looked horrified.

Di nodded. She had bought herself a new you-beaut camera. 'I could do that. Do you like your photos here on the wall?' she asked. They all agreed they did and Anna's sick feeling started to subside. 'I promise they'll look even better than those. And I'll show them to you before I send them. We just have to remember which clothes you bought there.'

'It's about time they had pictures of real women in ads,' declared Patsy.

'You mean, *old* women,' Kathryn added.

'We're still women. Just because we've lived a bit, doesn't mean to say we can't look good.' Patsy replied, 'and – we're about to live a whole lot more.'

'I still want to see the photos first,' Kathryn stated firmly, and Anna's head jerked up and down in agreement.

~ DI ~

Three weeks left, and I feel like pulling out. I can't go. I just cannot. Everybody else has somebody to share a room with and I don't. Always the odd one out – that's me.

Even when we had lunch at Kim's house, I felt out of place – disconnected. Imagine all those people on a cruise. But I need to go to write the stories we've promised the magazine. Of course, it costs extra for a single room – and they're often too small to swing a cat – if you had one in your bag – to let out – which I did! But in the end the money won't be a problem because the Travel Club has decided to split the funds equally across the package. So maybe they do want me to come. Bob says, of course they do – I must go. I wish he was coming but he's working full time at the agency while Peter's away.

I should be careful what I wish for. I wished for friends, and I had them and let them down. I wished I could travel again – and here I am going without really wanting to. And I wished I could be published and I got my wish – and all the other baggage that comes with it.

Three wishes from my fairy godmother and none of them turned out as I planned.

It was beginning to occur to Peter that with fourteen short days left, he was running out of time. The Travel Club had been in and out of the shop like cats on the wrong side of a door. You never knew when they would turn up and they always seemed to want Katy for advice. He wondered why he was going with them and not Katy. Then it occurred to him that she was needed right here.

He'd made progress with her. Gone out to dinner with her a few evenings and to the movies. He knew what she liked to eat now – a bit spicy, but not too hot. And what she liked to watch – much the same. Despite her outlandish exterior, she was a surprisingly old-fashioned girl. And he'd held her hand or casually put his arm around her in the pictures, and she'd snuggled up. But, somehow, he couldn't make the next move – whatever that was supposed to be. He was developing a plan, but so far it only extended to short-term stuff and every night she had some sort of appointment with one of the women or had to cook for her dad. Their social life had been put on hold and he was RUNNING OUT OF TIME.

'We need something more permanent,' he was muttering to himself as she walked into the agency on the Monday morning.

'Do we?' She sounded surprised and a bit miffed, then thought again and came over and perched her neat little bottom on his desk.

Peter had to back up on the creaky wheelie chair and look straight up over her short skirt, past her perfect little breasts and into her downcast eyes.

'Who's we?' she asked.

THIS WAS HIS MOMENT, he could feel the words elbowing their way up through his chest screaming to come out. He leaned forward, took her urchin face in his hands, opened his mouth to speak, thought better of it, closed it again, and instead pushed his lips up against hers, moving them gently. Her mouth was so red and soft, and willing and warm and just what he had imagined. He felt her hands on his shoulders drawing him forward and her longed-for lips open slightly under his as she pulled him towards her.

With a crack like a gunshot the glass door flew open, 'I cannot go,' Di declared – and Peter and Katy ignored her.

'DO YOU HEAR ME,' she yelled, stomping over to coupled pair, 'I REFUSE TO GO.'

Di grabbed Peter by the shoulder, wrenched him back still attached to the girl, and Katy promptly fell forward off the desk into Peter's lap.

Fascinating, thought Peter, I should have done this weeks ago, and then registered that some banshee was screaming behind his left shoulder. 'Go away,' he said, pulling Katy firmly into his arms, settling her onto his lap, and finding her mouth again.

'GO AWAY?! WHAT DO YOU MEAN GO AWAY? I'M NOT GOING ANYWHERE. THAT'S WHAT I'M TELLING YOU. I'M STAYING RIGHT HERE.' And Di sat, plonking her neat figure down on the floor right next to the occupied wheelie chair.

Had she conducted her tantrum in the proper fashion and laid down on the floor, the weight limit for the chair would have been visible and she may have moved sooner. The wheelie chair was groaning under its burden, just as its passionate passengers were groaning with pent up delight. Peter had bought the chair second-hand and it had travelled many kilometres backwards and forwards across the boards of the agency and could feel the end was near. The combined weight of the lovers was the final straw. Going to its death quietly, the chair's wheels folded up like a camel coming to earth, tipping Peter and Katy on the floor. The rest of its body disintegrated all over Di. The couple lay there, still hugging and laughing like loons as Di huffed and puffed back to her feet and stomped out of the shop.

'Wow,' said Katy as her breath returned. 'Fireworks.'

Gotcha, thought Peter. Hauling her to her feet he said, 'Better ring Bob.'

~ BOB ~

What an amazing group of women they are. A week to go before the trip of a lifetime – a bit cliché but true none the less – and they are getting things organised like professionals.

Katy is so impressive with all her lists – lists are such a comfort when you are doing something like this. Makes you feel like you know what you're doing, I always think.

I shared that with Di, who is not feeling so good. I wish I could go with her, but she needs to do this herself, and I need the work. I've told her she can ring me or text any time – any time at all. I feel like I got her into this with my deals with the magazine. But really, all I was trying to do was fix the problem she unwittingly caused. Yes. I do think it is unwitting because she really needs help with putting herself in somebody else's shoes. She looks so sad sometimes, but she lights up when I sit with her. That's what I need – to have somebody need me.

The Travel Club had one more meeting before they left for overseas. Everybody was there. Even Justin had study leave for his trials and promised he would work hard all the way there and back on the train. His mother looked sceptical at this, but his father was out of the country for the time being and she was reluctant to get into another showdown. How could he not be there, he reasoned with his mother, the women depended on him for coffee and tea and support. This was greeted by an eye roll from his mother. Had she noticed his results were better lately? Well, she had, but leaving the books behind for a day was not going to improve things. But nobody had books any more, just tablets, he had said, and he could easily take that on the train. Slippery as – like trying to nail jelly to a plate, she thought. But she understood him better recently and had been thinking about encouraging him to have a break and live a bit before he started any university course. What his father would make of that idea was anybody's guess – well, not really, it was her guess, and she was thinking the resulting argument wasn't going to be pretty. If she could trade Justin's trying harder with his HSC against a year working for Peter, that might bring calm and order to the house. She just needed to convince her better half – and Peter.

Justin was the last to arrive at the agency and they were going through the paperwork. The women had all brought their passports and Peter had their complete travel documents with copies for everyone. He had been tasked with carrying all the paperwork, including the passports. Katy had bought him a special bag to carry them and reminded him to keep them safely with him always. He had nodded at her, trying to stay on task and not be distracted by her luscious smile.

'How will we get to the airport?' asked Kim and Tam together, and then smiled at each other.

Bob had that covered. 'I've rented a twelve-seater bus with lots of room for the luggage and so we can all come out with you and say goodbye.'

Di beamed at him and reached for his hand under the table.

Kathryn's eyebrows rose, and Anna nudged her gently in the ribs.

Di was feeling much better since Bob had taken her out to dinner at the newest Italian place. As they shared pizza and pasta, Bob winkled all sorts of information out of Di about her past. She'd lived with a few men over the years but never had a permanent relationship. 'They all told me they needed to move on,' she had said, 'and I never really knew why. But there's no good flogging a dead horse – or partner for that matter.'

Bob just listened.

'After a while I found it easier not to get involved – and I'm happy with my own company. This Travel Club thing was unexpected.' She closed her eyes as she sipped her merlot. 'And it was okay for a while – but I'm so out of my depth with the trip. I really don't know what they expect of me.' Suddenly, her eyes were wide open boring into Bob's – searching for answers.

Bob was remembering that sweet desperation as he sat squeezing her hand under the table. He could see the looks on the faces of the other women and thought it was no bad thing for them to see that somebody loved Di – with all her spikiness. He had reminded Di about her commitment to writing for the magazine and how wonderful it would be for her if she could be published regularly. Along with this came a promise that she could contact him any hour of the day or night and he would be there for her across the world. He also planned to ask Elizabeth and Patsy to watch out for her.

'Thank you so much, Bob,' said Anna. 'A send-off like that will be lovely.'

And suddenly, he remembered how Anna had journeyed to the antipodes – without friend, or affection or farewell.

Anna had bought herself a new purple bag, which everybody was admiring. 'Such a luxury,' she said, 'I came here carrying one small suitcase with a change of clothes and everything else I owned I wore. Now look at me,' she gestured to the case, 'I could take all my clothes and Elizabeth's Molly in this, and nobody would notice the difference.' Molly's body shape had become quite the topic of conversation since they had heard she was off to boot camp.

'They might hear Molly howling every time food went by,' Elizabeth said, and laughter rippled around the room.

Peter heard Katy giggling and it warmed him through like a shot of espresso. There was nothing about her he could live without. No word that she spoke now that he did not hang on. No part of her that was not desirable.

Smitten, thought Patsy, you can smell the adoration like onions at a sausage sizzle. And it was coming from both sides of the table, circling around, and smacking everybody on the head. Peter and Katy were not looking at each other – no, they were not. They were sitting on opposite sides of the table so they could avoid touching – making it screamingly obvious that they were not looking at each other. And the women were not watching them closely – no, they were not. Patsy felt like rolling around on the floor with laughter.

'So,' said Katy, her glance circling the table and hurdling over Peter, 'have you got any more questions? Do you need us to do anything else for you?'

The women sat contemplating their lists.

Clothes – four of every layer – and some you can wear in the evening
A wrap – always comes in handy
Four pairs of pantyhose
Underwear and socks – six of everything

Waterproof Jacket
Sunhat – a folding one is best
Shoes – good walking shoes and something light
Wash kit and sunscreen
In your carry-on bag
Medication – check you have enough for the whole time and take your scripts
Make up
Camera
Spare undies
Purse and credit or debit card and some Euros
Copies of travel documents, passports, and itinerary

Elizabeth had visions of all her children's camp lists. What was missing were the NOs. No lollies. No toys. No alcohol – this addition when they were teenagers. It filled her with nostalgia and a longing to go back that knifed her through her ribs. She took a deep breath and practicality won out. 'We can always buy things when we get there,' she said firmly. 'It's not like we're going to the moon.'

Patsy was bouncing up and down on the chair next to her like an excited wallaby, and Di's hand tightened in Bob's in alarm. 'I can't wait to go shopping in Paris,' cried Patsy.

Katy heard Peter sigh and wanted to say, steady boy, steady, but she'd said that last night, and certainly didn't want to repeat it here.

'That room in your bag, Anna, will be good for shopping. All of you need to leave a bit of space for what you buy. You'll want to bring home souvenirs.' Katy was looking at each of them in turn. 'I take it you all have your Euros now?' They nodded back at her. She had given them strict instructions about how to do this with the bank and it had worked perfectly.

'What would you like us to bring back for you?' asked Kathryn.

Katy shook her head. 'No, no. This trip is for you. Spend your money on yourselves for a change. Make sure you enjoy yourselves, and have a good time. That's all I need. Come back happy and well.

That'll be my reward.'

Peter was staring at her – bemused, bewitched, and bewildered by her evolution into this wonderful caring woman. Of course, he had already thought she was wonderful in a purely physical way, but this other side of her, emerging like a butterfly from chrysalis, fired his heart.

'I'm sure we can find something lovely for you,' Patsy added, 'do you trust our taste?'

Katy just nodded, at a loss to respond.

'I'm guessing you're a size twelve?'

Katy nodded again.

'How exciting it'll be to shop for you!'

Suddenly, Katy realised that only Elizabeth, Kim, and Tam had someone to shop for.

Anna tapped Justin on the arm. 'And what would you like us to bring back for you?'

Justin was about to spit out the latest game for his Xbox, but caught Peter's eye, stopped, looked around at the eager grandmotherly faces and instead said, 'I take a medium in men's clothes and I wear lots of T-shirts. You all know what I like, you're my travel grandmas.' And the fire of shared love engulfed them all and soaked their eyes.

Nobody asked Bob, and he didn't mind at all, he had Di's hand firmly on his knee. Just bring Di back to me, ran through his mind, not knowing whether it was a thought or a prayer.

PART 2 - THE VOYAGE

CHAPTER NINE

~ PETER ~

Part of me wants to stay and the other part wants to bolt. Here I am conducting these wonderful women on a lifetime voyage and all I can think is: I wish my mother was here. Not for her, the joy of foreign shores beneath her feet, the best she could do was struggle from her bed to the couch and back – and that took all her strength. She used to winkle out of me every nanosecond of information about my travels. And she would ask me to repeat and repeat her favourite stories. Of course, some of them I had to edit – there are certain memorable things a man cannot tell his mother. How I wished I could show her the sights waiting for the Travel Club.

I shared this all with Katy last night as she snuggled in my arms. We had dinner at my place and, thankfully, Justin didn't turn up. As I cooked for her and we shared a bottle of wine, we chatted about the agency and then discussed Mum – and Katy kissed me when I cried. Then she told me about her nanna and I kissed her when she cried. And we held each other. What a temptation it was for us to peel of each other's clothes and seize the moment – and each other. Surprisingly, we agreed it would be most unwise to start something so committed when I was about to fly away.

It's a first for me, that she wants to talk about our relationship this way. I've slept with women before – before I became my mother's carer – but they were brief, one-night stands – exciting at the time. Come morning, they meant not much to me and, I suspect, less to the women. Sometimes I was drunk – and so were they – sometimes it was just – release. Once, while travelling, a woman said to me – let's get this sex thing over with and then we can be friends. So, we did – I cannot recall her name now. I became convinced that I wasn't very good at it. I mean, I got satisfaction and the women seemed happy enough in the moment – but who would know? Katy confided to me that she had only ever done it once in high school, when she was pressured into it by a boy. She had been physically hurt, mentally pained by his treatment of her afterwards – and gun shy ever since. So, I think I need to bone up – maybe not the right term – on my love-making skills. And the other important point is that I don't want to destroy our friendship. Yes, Katy arouses me completely, but we also love working together.

It feels slightly mercenary to put the agency into the equation, but, it would be madness to destroy our business relationship. There has to be a solution to holding this all together. Meanwhile, we have some time to think.

Elizabeth walked over from the Duty-Free checkout. 'Penny for your thoughts – well maybe a Euro – inflation and all, you know.' She wriggled in next to Peter. The thought flitted across his mind and burrowed deep under his heart that here was a woman who had been half of a long and seemingly joyful marriage. He had judiciously kept his head down while the Travel Club talked about the more intimate sides of their lives, but he'd heard enough to know that Elizabeth had loved John completely.

While Patsy had always shared very personal stories about her Ray, Elizabeth had lately started to reveal more about her relationship with her husband. Their work together at the church had joined them rather than causing friction, and occasionally he heard between the lines about how much love-making meant to them. Peter's own father had disappeared when the children were young, and he puzzled over what a happy long-term relationship might look like.

'Mmmm,' he smiled enigmatically down at her and patted her duty-free bag, 'what's in here?'

'Oh, just some perfume and lipstick. I found my favourites. John used to buy me L'heure Bleu and I haven't had any for ages.' She looked away over his shoulder, breathed deeply then added, 'And I love this colour lipstick.' She held it up for his approval.

He smiled at the conservative pink, nodded, then glanced around, 'Where are the others?' He felt the need to count heads. They had a couple of hours until the flight boarded but after passing through customs and security the solid weight of responsibility had borne down on him as the women scattered.

'They're fine,' Elizabeth touched his hand, still resting on the bag, 'It's okay. We're here to look after you.'

That's what he feared.

Six mothers.

A *ding* from his pocket made his stomach tighten. He pulled out his phone. Justin's picture appeared. He sighed. Not Katy then.

JUSTIN: *Wat r u doing?*

PETER: *I'm waiting at the airport.*

Ding!

JUSTIN: *I no. Wat r my grannies doing?*

PETER: *Shopping*

Ding!

JUSTIN: *Lol - R they excited?*

He had to think about that one. They might be – the women certainly seemed to be having a good time and they hadn't even left the country yet. Personally, his adrenaline was spiked by fear – fight or flight – you might say. He had been imagining all the terrible things that could happen. Sickness, accidents, abductions, terrorists, uprisings, plagues, death – he had dreadful daytime phantasies about all of the above and more. The truth was he feared losing one of them – one way or another. And losing them in a crowd was high on his list.

Ding!

JUSTIN: *R they smiling?*

PETER: *Probably.*

Ding!

JUSTIN: `U can't c them? Hav u lost them already?`

Peter almost went into the men's room and dropped his phone into the toilet, but he remembered he had given all the women his number as an emergency contact.

PETER: `Sorry, have to go, can hear flight called.`

Well, it was somebody's flight, not theirs yet.

Ding!

JUSTIN: `message me when u get there safely & give them my luv.`

PETER: `Sure.`

He felt a little guilty at his impatience with Justin. After all, Justin had only been showing his concern and caring.

He rose from the seat and, towing his carry-on, strode off in the direction of the shops, Elizabeth following in his wake. Travellers milled around him like exotic sea creatures in a tank. Pilots and stewards in smart suits and colourful uniforms wove their way through the clamour like sleek schools of fish. He watched the Malay airline women in their long, split batik skirts pass by and greet the middle eastern stewardesses with their pillbox hats and tiny veils, both groups wearing their cultures like a badge. What a melting pot, he thought, airports showed the deeply tribal nature of our world. Then he smiled to himself – and they also show how similar we all are. Everybody here needs to go somewhere, to eat, to drink, to look after those they love, to use the conveniences – as he walked past the line for ladies' room – to sleep, to care, and to be cared for. No matter age, sex, language or ability – they're all humans with the same human needs. And then the crowd in front of him opened and the formation of the rest of his entourage appeared – in pairs, towing their carry-on bags, beaming like excited fairies. All their aches and pains were wiped off their faces. They came towards him with steps springing – albeit slowly – surrounding his stilled figure.

'I know we're not who you really want to see, but here we are, reporting for duty,' pronounced Patsy, waggling her eyebrows.

Everybody laughed – including Peter.

'So, let's go find our departure gate, some coffee and the toilets – not necessarily in that order.' She winked.

They set off down the corridor, snaking through the mass of people, and he imagined they looked like a crew of their own – Six Sisters Airlines – or maybe She'll Be Right Airways. And then remembered the message. 'Justin sent his love,' he said to them all.

'We know,' they all chorused together, holding up their phones over their shoulders with Justin's picture and a row of kisses – and then broke down into giggles.

As their flight was boarding, his phone went *ding* again and he opened it to find a picture of luscious red lips pressed against a screen. He quickly sent back a heart emoji and floated down through the finger and onto the aircraft.

~ KATY ~

He's gone. 'Somewhere my love', Lara's theme is the soundtrack of my days. Well, twenty-one days' to be exact – maybe not quite as dramatic as Dr. Zhivago. I know Peter's not going into battle. Maybe a bit, but at least there's nobody trying to kill him. Unless he upsets the Six Sisters. How could he do that? Cut off their supply of cake? Ban them from shopping? Not talk about his private life? That would be me. Makes my belly melt to say that. And a bit hot down below too. Should he discuss me with them?

So, I'm asking myself if I mind if he tells Justin's travel grannies about our amour. That's what Peter called it the other night as we held each other. 'I don't want to have an affair with you. I want you to be my love, my amour,' he whispered against my lips, pulling me against him, rubbing his hands slowly from my shoulders down my back and over my butt. 'Now?' I asked thickly, feeling the heat trickle from my navel to my thighs. 'No – not now.' He was pulling me tighter and tighter against him – his body belying his answer. 'I want to go slow – and think about what we're doing.' Wrapped around me, he bowed his head and lay it down on my shoulder and we stood there like one being, soaking up the heat from each other.

I can't stop thinking about it. The further away he goes, the deeper he invades my brain.

The Singapore sun was slanting low through the tall windows, crimson on the nodding heads of the Six Sisters. Eight hours on board a plane was a long haul, but the women had settled into their seats and enjoyed the endless viewing of movies or TV series they had wanted to watch but never got around to. Having food served to them was a novelty too, particularly when breakfast came at dinner time. They had discussed all the fascinating details of their flight in the first hour of the five-hour stopover; exchanging facts about which movies were great and which were rubbish. Ooing and aahing over the sexy mini-series Patsy had found. Planning, Peter thought, to give it a look on the next flight.

After they had exhausted the topic he suggested they might all like to go for a walk through the airport and enjoy the orchid displays as it was the country's national symbol. Maybe they could do some more shopping. They were delighted with the little trolleys for carry-on luggage and set off like a mismatched team of sled dogs, in pairs, pushing rather than pulling their worldly goods. The next hour had been taken up with wandering around and then catching the airport train to the terminal where the Amsterdam plane was to depart.

Another meander around and Kathryn declared her legs were about to fall off and everybody agreed. They had settled down in the lounge at the departure gate, surrounded by their little trolleys like patient puppies, and were soon nodding in the warmth of the afternoon sun.

Peter snuck a photo on his phone and sent it back to Katy with the tag, *Sleeping Beauties*.

Ding!

Straight back came a selfie of Katy in bed with her head on the pillow.

KATY: *Your Sleeping Beauty.*

He sent back a heart.

Ding!

KATY: *How's it going, Prince Charming?*

PETER: *Good. Missing you*

Ding!

KATY: *me 2*

PETER: *How's the agency?*

Ding!

KATY: *I miss u squeaking backwards & forwards on your wheelie chair.*

PETER: *Anything else?*

Ding!

KATY: *Getting me coffee*

PETER: *And?*

Ding!

KATY: *Asking for my help on the computer*

PETER: *So Bob can do it all himself?*

Ding!

KATY: *Mostly. He's shown me a thing or 2.*

PETER: *As long as it's only business – not funny business.*

Ding!

KATY: *lol*

PETER: *Three weeks and we can create our*

own funny business.
Ding!
KATY: *lol*
PETER: *Guess I'd better wake up these ladies. They're calling our flight.*
Ding!
KATY: *Good night. Have a good flight. Think of me. xx*
PETER: *Always. xx*

Singapore to Amsterdam was fourteen hours. Kathryn tried to watch Patsy's mini-series but fell asleep half way through the first episode.

Anna leaned over and gently removed the headphones and turned off the screen. She could not sleep. Nor could she settle to watch anything. Her thoughts wove backwards and forwards across time and space, kaleidoscoping images of people and places like fractured glass.

Patsy and Elizabeth dozed together under blankets and eyeshades.

Kim slept on Tam's shoulder as he sat stiff-bodied and wide-eyed remembering other journeys.

Di – well, Di was so tightly sprung she felt she might never sleep again.

Peter relaxed as soon as the lights went down and tumbled into a wonderful dream, where Katy met him in an exotic airport dressed as Cleopatra, that left him trembling with pleasure.

When they landed, Peter lead his troupe through passport checks and down to the baggage carousel. He parked them all on a series of seats and went to find their luggage. The bags appeared like well-trained hounds readied for a dog show with the bright red spotty bows Katy had tied on the handles. As Peter heaved them off the conveyer belt, Tam collected them and towed them back to the women. He was taking his assistant job very seriously and Kim thought privately it was good for him to be needed. She was smiling at him across the crowded hall and he caught her glance and tipped his head sideways, grinning back.

By the time the bags were all stowed on trolleys and they were ready to leave, the women had visited the ladies', fixed their make-up and generally collected themselves. Out through the automatic doors the group chattered, Peter forging a path with a laden trolley and Tam guiding them from behind with another. Airports, thought Peter, must be the most evocative places in the world. They smell of coffee and onions and fresh bread – and grief and joy. He could see their travel company sign held up at some distance by a smiling young woman in a company uniform, with an older man and an Asian woman standing beside her. Peter turned towards the sign and Tam encouraged the women into formation. The women were wide eyed, their heads swinging from side to side, gobsmacked at the sights around them, trying to read Dutch. Tam and Kim had their eyes fixed on their daughter, who was next to the woman holding the sign – pulled like a magnet to their darling's face. She had surprised them with this welcome.

Peter was a man on a mission and had nearly reached the sign. Suddenly Anna stopped, and Tam had to throw his slight weight backwards to stop the laden trolley running her down. Her hand flew up over her mouth and she was reeling. Kathryn pawed at her friend's arm.

'Are you okay?'

Anna's head was nodding like it was loose on her neck.

'Are you sick?' asked Di. Anna's head was still wobbling up and down.

'What's wrong?' Elizabeth was holding her other arm.

'She's sick,' said Di, forbearing to add the *Der*.

'No, I don't think so,' Kathryn murmured. She was following

Anna's gaze to the stranger beside the sign.

'Does he look like his father?' asked Kathryn.

Anna's head changed direction, her gaze still fixed on the man who was now talking to Peter. 'No,' she finally whispered through the tears funnelling down her face, 'He looks like mine.' And the flood overtook her whole being, sweeping her back and forth over the years. They stood, waiting for Anna to recover, and while the world rushed past, the Six Sisters clustered around their friend, holding her up.

'Let's go and meet him,' Elizabeth finally said with the ebbing of the tide. Linking her hand through Anna's arm, as Kathryn did on the other side, they emerged from the congress. And so, with these two pillars of friendship supporting her on either side, and the strength of the others behind them, Anna walked forward to meet her past – and her future.

~ ANNA ~

My whole body is aching – like all my walls fell down and sent joy pounding through my old joints. It blurs all my other thoughts and makes me feel like dancing when I should be sleeping. It was so confusing at the airport. My son – YES, MY SON – came towards me palms outstretched and said, 'I'm Michael.' And took my hands in his long-fingers. 'I know,' I said, holding up our linked hands so we could look at them, 'I know.' Smiling at him, he laughed. 'I always think they are my dad's.' His English was very good. 'Actually, you got them from my dad. You are so like your grandfather. But,' I looked up fully in his face now, 'you have your father's chocolate eyes.' He let go of my hands then and wrapped his long arms around me – and I held my son for the first time – overwhelmed by the feel of him against me – and guilt that I ever let him go – and regret for all the empty years.

We travelled back here in the minibus, sitting next to each other, the heat of him against my arm and thigh. It brought back that brief moment when they lay him in my lap, the cord still attached, all those years ago. Then our rooms were ready.

I am laying on the hotel bed, Amsterdam beneath me, my son mine again – my body throbbing with pain – and happiness. I must rest now for a little. I feel the need to sleep but my brain is turning cartwheels like a schoolgirl. Kathryn counts herself to sleep, she says it relaxes her. As soon as I say one, I think what Michael must have been like at one, and two, and three – and it is too much to bear. Maybe I will just lay here and dream that I was with him for all those birthdays. And if I cry, I can count them tears of joy.

Peter lay in his room, sleep eluding him. Outside the lights of Amsterdam came through the open curtains – orange and yellow. And the music of the city – a rock band from the local city square, the explosive Dutch language of people on the street below, and the never-ending swish of bicycles on wet pavement.

Jet-lag, he thought, or just too much – too much talk, too much laughter, too much raw emotion, too much space between him and Katy. The distance was wringing his heart. Messaging and expensive calls were lovely but only made him want Katy here beside him – holding hands, laughing together, oohing and aahing over the foreign sights, shopping and – in his arms. Snatches of conversation and snapshot images from the evening drifted through his head.

The whole group had decided they would walk down to the local city square and have some Dutch food. They found a cosy pub that could accommodate the ten of them and settled down to enjoy the local fare. Michael proved to be a great asset as he could read and speak a little of the language. Anna sat beside him, proudly gazing at this man who had formed inside her. Across her face drifted expressions of joy and sadness, pride and wonder. Peter had never seen Anna like this before. Generally, she was quite a stern woman, with an air of despondency about her. But she was wearing her new holiday clothes and was alight with a nervous excitement. Peter saw Kathryn and Elizabeth anxiously glance at her every so often, and

Patsy shake her head a little as if her friend had shifted shape.

'What will you eat?' Michael had asked.

'We don't know.' The Travel Club chimed together. 'You order for us.'

'Do you like bitterbollen?' he suggested, 'they are meatballs and they come in different sorts.'

There was a rousing *Yes*. Kim, Tam and their daughter were joining in with the celebration, enchanted by being part of the festivities – and by being together. The waiter came then, edging his way between the tightly packed tables and suggested some other tasting plates they could all share. And what would they have to drink?

'Beer?' asked Peter and everybody else followed.

'Would you like Jenever with that?' the waiter asked, smiling at the non-plussed looks from everybody.

'Jenever, is gin with Juniper in it,' explained Michael, 'the Dutch drink it with beer. I have drunk it before and I like it.' There was a great discussion then, with much laughter, about gin being called Mother's Ruin and whether they would be able to find the hotel afterwards. In the end Peter ordered a few so they could all try it.

Maybe it was the Jenever keeping him awake, thought Peter, or the wishing to wake Katy up on the other side of the world and tell her about it: how Anna had changed; the flavour of bitterbollen; the hilarity over giant Nutella jar they had seen outside the pancake shop by the canal; the antique houseboats on the waterways; and how they had laughed their way back to the hotel, high on new sounds and scents and tastes and the joy of being together in this new place. His thoughts were more and more jumbled and he sent her a text that said 'Love yu', leaving his phone with a *ding* just as sleep overtook him and carried him away across the world.

CHAPTER TEN

The North Sea rain slanted down on the river ship as the women came aboard.

'I always wanted to travel on a barge, how romantic,' Patsy declared, delicately sheltering under a large umbrella held by a young crewman.

'I don't think they'd be happy to call it a barge.' Kathryn said, approving of the man's dapper uniform.

Anna tucked her hand in the crook of Michael's elbow, leaning lightly on him as they broached the gangplank.

Their pick-up from the hotel had been 2pm so that left the morning to wander around Amsterdam and see the sights. In pairs they had set off under a leaden sky, armed with street maps and cameras. They came back with stories of brimming cheese shops where you could taste the produce, and deep earthy perfumes of the flower markets where Kim and Tam had bought their daughter bulbs to grow in pots for her London flat. Peter had gone with Di, not wanting to lose her at the start of their trip, and come across the museum quarter with its stately buildings and formal gardens. She had a state-of-the art camera and he pulled her out of the way of pushbikes while she captured the city in two dimensions.

He was taking photos on his phone and sending them back to Katy, who was replying with emojis. Katy had offered to make a photo book of the holiday for the women and had asked them all to send her photos and stories. It would be an epic with all these pictures. Maybe it was epic anyway – legendary that these special women from an ordinary suburb could come all this way to support Anna's dream, and leave those around richer for the experience.

Anna and her son had sat in a coffee shop at the hotel, watching Amsterdam flow by, trying to wade together through a river of memories – and make sense of them.

'How do you make six old ladies say "shit"?' Peter was reading from the joke page on social media and the last word slipped out of his mouth before realised what it was. 'Sorry,' he added, eyes downcast, but Elizabeth's mouth wobbled with a furtive smile. It made her remember her young grandson who had rebuked his frazzled mother with *we don't say the shit in our family* – and feel lonely for him. The rest of the women raised their eyebrows.

'I know, I know.' Patsy shook her blonde locks and raised her glass of champagne. 'Yell "Bingo".'

Peter nodded, grinning now, raising his glass to her as the other women giggled around her. Champagne at 6 o'clock was good. No Bingo on board here – no need to swear. Instead, they were floating down the Rhine. Having left behind the leaning gabled houses of Amsterdam, they watched as the countryside paraded past them with its occasional windmills and wild-flowered meadows.

'Tell us another joke,' demanded Di, but Peter shook his head.

'Let's discuss what you can talk about at the Open Travel Club meetings on board.'

They all nodded thoughtfully. Part of their agreement was running open discussion groups over the journey. These would go for about an hour and a half and be at morning or afternoon tea time – just like at the agency.

'The first one we're having is my turn to introduce you all and talk about the Travel Club and how it began,' Peter explained. 'I think the company hopes that people might go back and start their own clubs to increase business.'

'It's a good idea,' agreed Kathryn, nodding sagely.

'Yes, it is,' replied Peter, 'although, it could never be like our Travel Club.' And suddenly he had an epiphany. It belonged to him – and Katy – and Justin – and Bob – as much as it belonged to the Six Sisters. Warmth rose in him.

'I've asked Elizabeth, Anna and Kim to help me with this.' The three women smiled and nodded back at him. 'We've agreed that I will ask them questions about themselves and their lives and how it all started.'

Katy had suggested this when they discussed the boat sessions. 'You have to start somewhere, and people love to share stories,' she'd said, 'and if you ask the women about themselves. Where they lived? What they were doing at the mall? What was it about the travel agency that attracted them? All sorts of other things will come out that other people could identify with. Then you can move on to the specific places.'

That was the second thing the cruise company wanted. With their tours available all over the world, the management had decided they could run a video of various places and the women could then talk about their visits there. They could answer what they knew, with a professional tour guide to fill in specifics of current tours. If they got stuck the tour guide would ask some questions to elicit information. More than that, the company wanted the women to mix and get to know the other clients and promote the wonder of travelling. Peter explained this to the women and they toasted him, champagne glasses raised – it would be great to talk.

'Do any of you feel shy about it?' he asked the group.

'A bit,' said Elizabeth, looking around for support, 'but I think we can all help each other.'

Nods all round.

'We're here for one another.' Patsy added, and Elizabeth took her hand,

'Thank you,' Elizabeth smiled.

'And we can enjoy our holiday. I can't wait for all those musicians on the program,' Kathryn enthused, lifting her glass. 'Bottoms up.' She saluted and they all laughed and echoed her toast.

The glass door swung back, and Katy and Bob looked up from their computers. The hairdresser from down the mall, sashayed in.

'How's it going?' she asked.

'How's what going?' Katy looked back down at the screen. A number of interesting *its* were spooling through her brain.

'You know, the holiday.'

'We have lots of holidays here,' said Bob, 'which one would you like?' He rose from the chair and pointed her in the direction of the display wall. 'In Australia? America? Europe? Africa? How about Iceland? Iceland's very popular at present.'

The hairdresser's eyebrows rose towards her bouffant fringe. 'Is he for real?' she turned to Katy with her chin pulled in as her eyebrows fell.

'You're in a travel agency.' Katy was still looking studiously at the screen.

'I mean the Travel Club – you know – and Peter,' the stylist waggled her eyebrows suggestively at Katy who thought they looked like caterpillars.

'They've all arrived safely,' Bob butted in as Katy was staring at the hairdresser, 'and are aboard the river ship.'

'And?'

'And what?' said Katy

'Are you going to share their stories? And their pics?'

'What a good idea.' Katy was rising to her feet as the hairdresser backed up. 'Come back tomorrow and I'll put something up on the screen. And,' she snatched two of the brochures from Bob and thrust them out, 'have a squiz at these and when you're finished with them give them to your clients.' The hairdresser nodded her way out the door.

'I'll be back,' she muttered.

'I'm sure you will,' answered Katy to the slam of the glass door, and she and Bob were rocking on their chairs with laughter.

CHAPTER ELEVEN

From: Elizabeth
To: Katy
Subject: Day 1

Hi Katy

Hope all is well for you. As promised I am sending you some photos. We have decided to take turns to email you and I get to be first!!!!

Amsterdam is the most fascinating place. There are bicycles everywhere and they even have tripled decker storage racks for them. We went out yesterday morning for a walk around and had to watch out we didn't step into the bike lane on the footpath and get swept away. Some of the cycles have long bodies with seated boxes on the front so parents can take their children shopping in them. It would be hard if there were hills, but everything is so flat here. Everybody is so fit from riding.

The Travel Club

Patsy and I went together and found the cheese shops and flower markets. She was also fascinated with the explicit pictures and carvings in some of the tourist shops. Better not share that with the rest of the mall. Really!!! Delft porcelain privates with blue flowers on them – who would have thought! I preferred the blue and white pottery cow. Patsy laughed at the sign asking people not to ride it. And Patsy wants to go into a café because we have been told they sell marijuana there rather than coffee. I refuse. This place is surreal enough undrugged. On the way back to the boat we stopped at an old windmill Vermeer had painted. I feel like I am travelling through an art gallery.

Although it has been raining – quite common for Amsterdam I am told – we are having a lovely time on board. For our first night we had the most hilarious safety talk by the Hotel Manager, Hans: Where the life jackets were and so on – and boat stations. Although they told us that most of the time we were in such shallow water that if we fell overboard we could just walk ashore. He also filled us in on the use of those wipes that say they are disposable and block up whole boats' toilet systems. I have put mine away as I am sure half the boat has – we old women know about blocked toilets and NO we do not want one.

Jeanie Wood

This morning we took a canal boat cruise around Amsterdam. The rain came off and on, but we were well protected by the glass roof as we travelled around its huge canal system. The city is built on piers into swamps and, on the coast, there are dykes to hold back the North Sea and windmills to pump the water. Most of the Netherlands is marsh country that has been drained. For centuries life here has been a constant fight against nature. The houses have roofs like milk-maids' hats and many are leaning drunkenly sideways because of the shifting foundations in the boggy ground. Old boats and barges line the canals as houseboats with garden areas, chimneys and the occasional dog to bark at the passing flotilla – yes, I am missing my Molly, even her woofing. We passed Anne Frank's house on the tour and I wondered at how such a beautiful place could have experienced such terror.

At night we attended the Captain's Welcome Cocktail party and all the women on board were presented with long-stemmed roses. Attached is a photo of us in our finery holding our roses. Thank you for helping us choose nice outfits for nights like this. I suspect it has been a long time since any of us have dressed up and I felt like Cinderella – off to the ball. On the edge of my mind was John's voice telling me I looked a treat.

Michael escorted Anna in and I have never seen her look so beautiful – glowing with pride on her son's arm. Peter was dashing in his suit. Wow I didn't know he had one. Did you help him buy it?

At the party, the passengers were introduced to the crew and then they announced us – The Travel Club they called us, and then by our names. I felt like a film star – then it occurred to me that we would have to sing for our supper. Guess I'll learn to do that.

~ ELIZABETH ~

Patsy and I are taking turns to catch up with our emails on the computer in the cabin. I sent one to my family first – here safe and sound – having fun. *Then I wrote one for Katy and attached some photos. I told her all about our adventures – well some of them – writing about Patsy in the souvenir shop was a bit tricky. I could hardly write what she whispered in my left ear: 'Oh look – a porcelain penis – a Delft dick – a ceramic stiffy.' Getting louder with each euphemism. Sh, sh I was saying but I could feel the laughter boiling up inside me. It was the blue flowers that got me – so old fashioned and decorative and incongruous. Patsy held a sample up in her hand to me and said, 'Oh, come on Liz, you know what it is. How many kids have you got? How many kids have they got? I'm sure you've seen plenty.' By that stage, the two young shoppers behind us were snorting with laughter. And I couldn't help myself. 'Why, yes, I have,' I whispered, 'and I have not forgotten what it is – despite the fact any I have been... um... familiar with... were lacking in forget-me-nots.' And we both broke up in the shop, our laughter bandaging – and in some ways relieving – the open wounds of our lives. Patsy bought two penises, one for me and one for her. 'To remember,' she said, without saying what it was we were remembering.*

The lounge was dim and warm with soft piano at one end, as the Travel Club sipped their coffee. The lights of Amsterdam reflected off the water outside and water traffic plied up and down with the business of the river, and the water silvered in the twilight.

'Let's play a game,' suggested Elizabeth, 'I play this with my grandchildren. You have to say what was the best thing about your day.'

Kim and Tam began by talking about the flower markets and the bulbs they had bought for their daughter. 'So, she will remember us when we are across the world from her,' finished Tam

'I wish we could take some back for my garden,' said Patsy.

'Never make it through Customs.' Peter shook his head. 'Those little beagles would have you in one sniff.'

'They wouldn't flower at our place anyway. Tulips like cold climates,' declared Di.

'I could grow them in the fridge.' Patsy laughed

'I'll ask my daughter to take pictures of them when they bloom and send them to us,' Tam said, patting Patsy's hand. 'You could print them and put them around your garden.'

'That's the sort of gardening I like.' Elizabeth was grinning at Tam.

'How about you?' Kim asked Patsy.

Elizabeth and Patsy exchanged an eloquent look. Peter noted the interesting flush rising up Elizabeth's neck. Patsy opened her mouth to answer and Elizabeth quickly put in, 'souvenir shopping,' and left it at that.

Patsy added helpfully. 'I wanted to go into a coffee shop, but Elizabeth wouldn't let me.'

'She wanted to try a joint,' said Elizabeth, raising her eyebrows.

'You should try everything once,' stated Patsy.

Peter privately thought she probably had.

'As if you've never done it before,' answered Elizabeth.

'Not in Amsterdam.'

The whole group applauded.

Peter glanced around the room. The other passengers were looking at them and smiling at their laughter. Now to come up with his favourite thing.

CHAPTER TWELVE

From: Kathryn
To: Katy
Subject: Day 2

Hi Katy,

Last night we left Holland behind. I was tempted to sing everybody Tulips from Amsterdam as we sailed away but desisted. Today we enjoyed a walking tour of Cologne. The rain mostly held off although there was a cool breeze. Anna and her son joined the slow walkers' group under one umbrella, so Di and I teamed up with Elizabeth and Patsy and really enjoyed one another's company.

This town has its own unique flavour, sitting so close inside the border with The Netherlands and France. The buildings are bright coloured along the waterfront but have steep gables rather than the distinctive Dutch hat shape. In the main square there were also Roman ruins with the original gate of the Roman town and a window in the walkway down to some archaeological diggings from those times.

Medieval laneways lead up to the Cathedral which looms over the town with its massive Gothic spires, black with centuries of grime, they look like rusted lace. Carvings everywhere – as you walk through the doors the saints' frozen faces peer down on you as a reminder of faithful humanity. Inside there was a suspended organ – I would love to play it. Imagine climbing up there, although the keyboard is probably down on the ground somewhere. There was gold everywhere – especially the box containing the relics of the Three Wise Men. Stolen, of course, and then taken from thieving Milan to here as a gift. And I loved the reclining bishop statues on the tombs. Up on one elbow, as if they had one last admonition to the assembled throng, before they popped off.

This afternoon was the first meeting of the Open Travel Club. Peter led the discussion and told everybody about how we began in the local coffee shop and moved to the agency. You got quite a few mentions – and he gets such a sweet look on his face when he talks about you. He showed some pictures of the agency – you know the ones you took at our last meeting – and he had *some of you and Bob and Justin too. Quite a few of you actually.*

Elizabeth took over then and talked about how she had met Anna and then Kim and they had formed a friendship because they liked to talk about travel. The audience loved it when she got them all on their feet – some struggling and played a game of 'where have you been?' which involved standing until she named a place you had not been and then you had to sit down. Wow some of the folk had travelled far and wide. Anna and Kim followed this and talked about leaving behind their countries and the memories they carried with them. All of this was accompanied by magnificent afternoon tea.

In the evening went out to Namedy Castle at Adenach for dinner. It was magnificent, although the banks of deer antlers high in the entrance way were a bit overwhelming. During our tour I was permitted to play two wonderful old Bosendorfer grand pianos. My favourite Chopin Nocturne jumped into my head and flowed out my fingers. Bliss. We had dinner in the antique dining room with late sun streaming through long windows. I LOVED hearing a performance by a Master's student on the piano – a new Yamaha with a bright hard tone- give me the old Bosendorfers any time.

The Travel Club

From: Di
To: Bob
Subject: Photos

Dear Bob,
So far, so good. The new camera works a treat – really worth the investment. While the rest of the TC take pictures of the scenery, I take pictures of them – in the scenery. I have been showing them around every night and the rest of the group are delighted. The best ones are of Anna and Michael. I am attaching a photo at the dinner, Anna watching Michael talking to other guests, amazed. And today walking through the Cathedral the rainbow light from the stained glass illuminating their faces. As I passed them, I realised they were praying hand in hand. Thanking God, I think, so I turned and took some pictures from a distance with the windows and the cross behind them. When I come home I might write a novel and call it the Prodigal Mother – what do you think?

'Have you seen Di's photos?' Justin said.

He had managed to come over to the agency for the afternoon because Katy didn't answer often enough when he texted her. Eventually he got frustrated and decided to come from school on the train and tell his mother he had been in the library. He didn't really expect his mother to believe him, but it was a reasonable enough excuse to deflect her criticism. As the train rocked along he had done some study for the assessment task coming up – so, he reasoned, you could call the train a library. Come to think of it, this actually helped him study. At home the Xbox drew him like a snake charmer.

'Beautiful, aren't they,' answered Bob.

'Trouble is,' said Katy, 'we're too busy running the agency to do anything with them. And I have this as well.' She showed Justin Elizabeth and Kathryn's emails. 'I planned to put the photos and some of the text together up on the screen for all our visitors. But I just don't have time.'

'What visitors?' Justin was glancing around, it seemed quiet enough.

'Well, the hairdresser for a start, then there's our friendly butcher, and the two brothers who own the DVD store, not to mention every other person that works in the mall,' she was building up steam now, 'and every single person who's ever visited the Travel Club.'

As she finished, two women in aprons stuck their heads in the door, raised their eyebrows and backed away as she vigorously shook her head and scowled at them.

'It seems everybody wants to enjoy the Travel Club's holiday,' she finished.

'What about Bob?' Justin asked.

'What about Bob? He's doing Peter's job and he's flat out too. All this publicity is bringing in the business.'

Bob was nodding in agreement.

'What about me?' Justin looked her straight in the eyes.

'What about YOU?' She was flabbergasted. 'YOUR MOTHER would murder you – and me – if you did this instead of your school work.'

'O.K.' He was thinking out loud he realised, 'what if I did this as well as my school work, instead of playing on the Xbox?'

Katy gaped.

Miracles do happen, thought Bob, a streak of warmth rising from his gut, they're amongst us all the time. We just need to recognise them – and be grateful.

Katy was too astonished to think anything. It would help. It could also be a DISASTER. What the heck. 'Well, you can't come here every afternoon. Why not put together a presentation for us now with what we have and then you can talk to your mum and she can ring me. I could set up a drop box and put them all in and you can work from home. But not too much time. I don't want to endanger your HSC.'

Jumping onto Peter's abandoned computer, he began to put together the site. Endanger his HSC, he mused, at one stage his HSC had been a joke. It was getting more and more serious all the time. If he could pull off working here and doing reasonably at school that *would* be a miracle. Maybe then he'd be allowed to follow his uncle into the agency.

KATY: *Justin is helping us put up the Travel Club story on the big screen.*

Ding!

PETER: *What! I am going to be in so much trouble with my sister.*

KATY: *He says he's doing it as well as schoolwork.*

Ding!

PETER: *Sure he is.*
KATY: *His mother has agreed.*

Ding!

PETER: *Wow. How did you do that?*
KATY: *He did it.*

Ding!

PETER: *Now I believe in miracles.*
KATY: *LOL*

CHAPTER THIRTEEN

From: Patsy
To: Katy
Subject: ay 3

You know all those posters of medieval castles on the Rhine you have on your wall? We sailed past them this morning through the Rhine Gorge. They might look ROMANTIC, but they were basically toll booths where various noblemen extracted taxes from the river traffic. Sometimes they kidnapped people and held them to ransom if the travellers looked wealthy enough. The size of the castle is related to how much money the robber barons could extract. It's a pity they can't still do it. It might be fun to live in a castle for a bit and I'm sure there are some rich people on these river tours.

You wonder how they built such sprawling fortresses up there on the tops of the hills

– there's a bit to be said for the feudal system – all those peasants. And for that matter it amazes me how fast the toll collectors could get down their hillsides to catch and tax the boats.

Along the shore there are villages with beautiful gardens, stone watch towers and churches – in one place you have to walk through the pub to get to the church – Ray would have loved that. And the modern river traffic is huge – all sorts of barges with food, and gas, and building materials – with little cars on the back so the people who live aboard can get around on shore. Now that would be a romantic life.

There are vineyards marching up and down the hillsides that have been there since Roman times. They look like fields that have been combed. Some have been abandoned but most are still green and blooming. I wonder if I could grow grapes in my garden. It must be tricky to work on these vines on such a slope. Kathryn asserted that all the workers in the vineyards had one leg longer than the other. That made me laugh and I saw Di trying to work the joke out until Kathryn explained it.

We passed the Lorelei Rock and Kathryn sang us a song she had learned in High School – evidently the legend said it was where a siren sat, combing her locks and luring *sailors to their deaths. Maybe the water was too deep to walk to shore there – or one of their legs was too short. Lol. As we passed the rock we were served Rudesheimer coffee – very alcoholic before noon. But one has to keep up. You will be pleased to know we are all getting on fine. Together we walk and talk and laugh and drink and eat and sometimes shed a tear – like sisters.*

Seated around a table in the middle of the top deck, Peter and Michael were sipping their coffee. 'How's it going with your mother?' Peter lifted his chin towards Anna, who was standing by the rail among the group of women all looking at the shore and chattering like sparrows.

'Good, I think,' answered Michael, 'we are taking it slowly, but she seems happy – and so am I.' He glowed as he looked across at Anna.

'After all these years it must be hard to think of her as your mother,' Peter said.

'Not really. I always hoped we would find each other. My Papa and Mama told me I was an adopted child – and that my parents were too young to look after a baby. So, all my life I've thought a lot about my real mother and father. After Mama died, Papa encouraged me to find my family.'

'Sounds like you had great parents.'

'Yes. I was lucky… luckier than Anna, I think. What about you? Do you still have your parents?'

Peter took a large swig of the coffee, breathing deeply to hold back the choking as the fumes of alcohol rose up his nose. He slowly shook his head. 'No, my Dad left us when I was a baby and Mum died a couple of years ago. I was her carer over the last few years.'

'You were lucky then – you were able to spend time with your mother.'

Peter considered this statement. Most people in his country would have seen it as an imposition on a young man to care for a disabled relative – even his mother. It was as if the world suddenly shifted perspective and he acknowledged that he had indeed been fortunate to have that time. His gut twisted that he had never seen things from this side before – life was always comparative. He couldn't contemplate those years with his mother without sadness and his focus flinching away. 'Yes, I guess I was… fortunate.' He took another big swig. Restorative, he was thinking. 'And now I feel lucky being with the Travel Club.'

Michael noticed the shifting emotions across Peter's face and smiled, happy to go with the new topic, 'They keep you busy.'

Peter just nodded, thinking his new-found friend didn't know the half of it. The women were heading back towards them, jettisoning their empty coffee cups on the table in front of him.

'Wow that coffee was strong,' Kathryn huffed.

'We're well-oiled now,' said Patsy

'I hope we can walk straight,' Elizabeth added.

'You can hang on to me,' Peter stood and offered his arm.

'I'll need an afternoon sleep,' Kim was looking playfully at Tam who raised his eyebrows.

Di was snap, snap, snapping with her camera.

CHAPTER FOURTEEN

From: Anna
To: Katy
Subject: Day 4

This morning we had a glass blowing demonstration by three generations of a family who had escaped from East Germany during communist times. They took hardly any tools – just knowledge and one another. Their work is beautiful, and they are so lucky to all still be together as a family.

We have started travelling along the Main River with its thirty-two locks varying in depth from 2.75 to 6.30 metres. Michael is so excited. He told me all the details and wrote it all down. In fact, all the men were out on the front of the boat taking lots of photos as we went through the first lock. The captain closed the sundeck and the swimming pool, and the wheelhouse was lowered flat, so he could steer under the low bridges.

In the afternoon we wandered around Miltenberg with its red and white Franconian flags. The town is between the river and the hills with half-timbered houses dating from the 12th century. There were flowers in all the window boxes and the sun shone down on the village square with its glittering fountain as I sat sipping coffee with my son. My favourite place was a local wine cellar built into the hillside. Hope you like my photos.

~ ANNA ~

I feel like crying all the time and I can't tell whether its joy or grief. This morning the glass was like jewels and I bought some for gifts for my family – how exciting to say my family *– in Vienna. Michael told me what each of his children would like. My heart welled up inside me with the thought that I had* family *to buy a gift for. And, of course, I bought one for Katy as well.*

The glass blower's story burned like a blue-flamed torch, dividing my heart in my chest. I struggled alone to make a new life in a new country and lost my history. Michael has so much he wants to know – about me and my family – about his father and his family – about generations of ancestors I have purposely forgotten. When we talk he turns on his phone and records us – so we will regain the past, he says, and capture the present. But some of it's hard to say. The past is a foreign country, I have heard a writer who said, they did things differently then. I am afraid to tell him everything because, by today's standards, my family seems cruel and heartless. But it was the way things were done, and expectations then were different. It was understood that girls would give up their babies to spare the family shame and to give their children a better chance. Michael tells me he has had a wonderful life with the best of parents. There was no way I could offer him all his adoptive parents did. So why do I still feel guilty?

'Have you been on my site?' Justin asked Bob. He had managed to sneak away from school again. Since his mother would be late home and his father was still overseas, he had calculated he could spend two hours at the agency in the late afternoon and two hours there and back study-travel. This was his new term for a personally radical concept – although anything regarding study was a radical concept. It was possible to do the work remotely, but he actually enjoyed being with Bob and Katy as he put it together and, astonishingly, his school work was improving with the focused study on the train.

Bob nodded. 'Di sends me pics each evening, I'm putting them together for her with a bit of an itinerary, so she can write her story for the magazine.'

'Has she written some already? Can I use it?'

This time Bob shook his head. 'She has written some, but no, you can't use it. The magazine has exclusive rights to it.'

'The thing is…' Justin considered the photos on his screen, 'the travel grandmas are sending a diary – and some of their photos – and they're good, but Di is capturing their stories in their faces. Have you seen this one?' Justin turned his screen and Bob wheeled across on his chair. It was a photo of Anna, straighter than he remembered her, standing in a group by the rail, with those trademark castles in the background. Anna's gaze was on something much closer than the towering strongholds or even the vineyards that marched up and down the hillsides; she was looking slightly sideways, intent on the conversation between the two men sipping coffee in the middle of the boat. Her face held so much longing and pride that Justin felt like crying just to witness it. It made him wonder if his mother had ever looked at him like this – or if she ever would – and to imagine what he could do to make her gaze like Anna's.

'Put that photo up,' said Bob, 'for those who know Anna and will be glad to see her so happy.'

'Is Di's article going to be Anna's story?' asked Justin.

'Partly,' replied Bob, 'and all the other stories, as well.'

'When Di published that other one in the magazine I thought… well, I didn't really like her. But now I realise she is a bit different – but brilliant.'

'Yes, she is,' said Bob, smiling to himself, warm inside, 'brilliant.'

CHAPTER FIFTEEN

From: Kim
To: Katy
Subject: Day 5

Today is my wedding anniversary. Tam and I have been married for forty-four years. How wonderful to enjoy it on such a holiday. We docked at Wurzburg today and a coach drove us from there to Rothenberg through farming country with maize and sugar beet and all sorts of fruit. The farms are small villages and they keep their livestock in huge barns all through the winter and only let them out in summer on Dancing Cow Day. Rothenberg is a medieval town with gingerbread houses, cobbled streets and an original wall to keep out invaders – but not tourists. That's good. In the main square there was a couple getting married outside the registry office. The whole wedding party was in local dress – the women's is called a Dirndl and the men's

Lederhosen. They looked very beautiful. There were white doves all around the square as if they were in the wedding party. Tam and I congratulated them and said today was forty-four years for us. Patsy told them we were the wedding crashers, but the couple smiled at us all – maybe they did not understand what we said.

Afterwards we visited a Christmas Shop and bought some decorations for our grandchildren – so pretty just like Santa's cave.

When we got back to our room on the boat the bed was decorated with a pair of swans made out of our towels and rose petals on the bed. Tam had told them about our Anniversary.

After lunch we walked around beautiful Wurzburg with its baroque churches and bridge full of statues defending the town. Then we enjoyed a celebration dinner with all our friends in the special restaurant. I have had such a lovely day.

~ KIM ~

That was us – I said to Tam – not much more than children, married in the village. And when those young people made those promises do they know what they are doing? Not really, and neither did we. Did we love each other as we do now? I don't know. We have been through so much together – for better and for worse – but nobody thinks how bad worse can be before it gets better. Still, we must have loved each other a lot to plan a lifetime together. Of course, marriage changes over the years. But we didn't think about that on our wedding day, and I guess the *couple we saw today were not thinking about it either.*

The restaurant at the back of the vessel was reserved for fine dining. Tam had managed to secure a table for nine for his wedding anniversary. He had considered whether he would take Kim out to dinner on their own but decided that, since the Travel Club was sharing this journey, it would be good for everybody to celebrate with them. Setting up a table for nine had been challenging in the small area, but the staff had managed to put together two tables with another seat on the end. So, the nine sat elbow to elbow trying not to jostle each other – just like family.

Peter carefully rose holding his full champagne glass, 'Happy Anniversary,' wishes echoed around the table as he took his seat again.

'Thank you so much,' said Tam, 'We are so happy you can be with us on this special day.'

'Thank you for inviting us,' offered Elizabeth, 'we are very privileged.'

'You are like sisters to me,' Kim smiled at each of the women around the table, 'and you,' she motioned towards Peter with her glass, 'like a son.'

Was it okay for men to cry, wondered Peter, wishing one more time that both his mother and Katy were with him. Maybe they were.

'Tell us how you met,' said Patsy.

Kim smiled. 'I got him on the black market.'

Everybody laughed.

'I mean it,' she said, 'it was hard to buy things in Saigon and the black market was very useful.'

'And you are still *dealing* with the consequences,' Patsy came back and there was more laughter.

'I was not too expensive,' stated Tam. More mirth. 'And I have lasted well.' Hilarity all round.

'What's your secret for a long marriage?' asked Kathryn

'Always agree with your wife,' said Tam, straight-faced. 'And tell her how beautiful she is.' Now sighs passed from one to the next.

'Seriously though,' said Kim, 'we just kept our promises. We said we would stay together and be faithful all our lives and that's what we have tried to do. We taught our children that marriage is for ever but that you had to keep loving and not just put up with each other.'

'Sometimes I have to put up with her,' said Tam and Kim playfully tapped him on the back of his veined hand.

'Good that you have,' answered Kim, 'otherwise you would have missed out on all this.'

And everybody applauded.

'But I wanted to say,' said Tam rising to his feet, 'in front of everyone today is how blessed we are to have each other to love.' And Kim stood and turned into his arms.

'A toast all round,' said Peter rising to his feet again, 'To Tam and Kim.'

Everybody stood then, wriggling out of their chairs, raising their glasses, 'To Tam and Kim,' they chorused,

'To love,' whispered Anna – and Peter caught the ghost of her words and swallowed them deep into his belly.

'To love,' he murmured into the fizz buzzing in his head.

Elizabeth excused herself and went to 'find the Ladies'.

'Think I might go too.' Patsy swanned off behind her.

Peter watched them go and it suddenly hit him that this might make them feel sad. He knew they missed their husbands. But they returned shortly afterwards, arms linked and make-up fresh.

'Are you okay?' he whispered to Elizabeth as she sat back next to him.

'I'm fine.' She gulped her wine.

Should he? He might be on sticky ground. He felt sick at the thought of making her cry – again – he felt sure she had before. What would Katy say? Out it came, 'You must miss John.'

Elizabeth's eyes sprang open to hear her beloved's name from a young man who had never known him. It hit her that she must talk a lot about her husband. Peter heard her swallow. She nodded and took a deep breath.

'Yes, I do. But I'm so glad for Kim and Tam to have this day. John and I had many like it.' A huge sigh rose unbidden from just below her heart and she swallowed again in that painful way. 'We always thanked God that He had joined us and if He has separated us, then that's what is meant to be. I loved my marriage, and I will always love John, but now I'm blessed with more God-given days to enjoy. And,' she said sat up tall in her seat and raised her glass in salute, 'I mean to.'

Peter felt so many questions bubbling up inside him, 'How did you know you were meant to be together?'

Elizabeth slowly shook her head, 'I don't think we did. We were friends first and then… Then I guess we fell in love. And it wasn't always easy – marriage isn't – but we believed in being faithful and kind and loving each other – just like Kim and Tam – so we stuck together. And it brought us so much joy. Here's to love.' She clinked her glass on his.

'To love,' he repeated – and wondered why his father had left his mother.

CHAPTER SIXTEEN

From: Di
To: Katy
Subject: Day 6

Our second Open Travel Club was held this morning. I had helped them put together a photo presentation from old slides and it brought out lots of other stories from passengers about former travel. Patsy talked about travelling around Europe in a camper in the seventies when she and Ray were young, and Kathryn talked about touring Europe as a young musician. The consultant had current photos matching some of the places and was able to discuss modern travel.

We are in Bavaria now, so the ship served beer and bratwurst for Fruhschoppen – I think that means morning tea. We sat around chatting to passengers as we slurped beer.

I have found my favourite place in the whole world – Bamberg. It is like a fairy-

tale town with houses and streets built among rushing water under convoluted bridges. The town hall - Rathausen - is built in the middle of the river and there was a beer festival happening all through the town. Lederhosen and dirndls were everywhere, and people were raising their frothing steins and consuming all sorts of sausage. It looked like Oktoberfest in Rivendell (my favourite place from the Lord of the Rings Movie). This is a place that makes you want to come back and stay.

From: Bob
To: Di
Subject:Bamberg

Dear Di,

So, Bamberg is on our bucket list now. I have never been there, but it sounds wonderful. I am creating a schedule for us - maybe - No pressure.

When Carol's phone rang in the middle of the night, she presumed it was her husband.

'Hello darling,' she murmured, heavy-voiced, half drugged by sleep.

'Oh, hi Carol, it's Peter.'

She jerked up from her bed. 'What are you ringing for? Do you know what time it is? Are you okay?' The last question was rapid, as she suddenly registered the singularity of this long-distance call.

'Yeah, I'm fine. Just felt like chatting,' he realised he had only answered two of her questions.

Never, well hardly ever, had Peter wanted to chat to her – even when their mother was dying he had mostly kept his thoughts to himself. 'O.K,' she snuggled back down under the covers, 'forget the time. What did you want to talk about?'

'Uh… well… um…'

This could go on all night, thought Carol. 'Tell me, how's the holiday going?' This was safe ground – she hoped. 'Nobody fighting? Injured? Dead?'

'No, no, and no – it's great. We're all having a great time and the Travel Club are experts at the chat sessions.'

'Well, they do love to talk.'

'Yeah, they've turned out to be professional talkers. The crowd loves 'em.'

Carol laughed. 'And are *you* enjoying the holiday.'

'You know – I am. The women are great company, and I'm enjoying sharing a room with Anna's son Michael. We often yack late into the night and cover all sorts of things – and of course, we're sailing through the most spectacular scenery and incredible towns.'

'Good for business, I expect,' said Carol. 'Seeing everything. You should travel more often so you can promote what you've experienced.'

'That's true.' There was a dead silence.

Carol filled the gap. 'Did you hear Justin's been going into the agency?'

Oh no, thought Peter, now I'm in for it. 'Yeah, Katy told me.' He took a deep breath. 'How's that working out?'

'Better than you might think. He's actually studying more because he has to be more organised – and, I suspect, because he can't take the

Xbox on the train.'

'Does his dad know?' This was the critical question. If Gary found out when he got home from the business trip, fire and brimstone would rain down on Justin's slippery shoulders. And Carol might be burned in the downpour.

'Yes, I've told him. He wasn't happy, but, since he's seen Justin's latest school results, he's decided it might be all right. I think he's coming to terms with the fact that his son will never be a rocket surgeon. You know, in the end, we both just want him to be happy with what he does.'

'I know,' replied Peter, 'and he certainly makes everybody happy at the agency.'

'How did the reunion with Anna and Michael turn out?'

'Fantastic. Just beautiful really. Anna is so proud of him. And Michael's been hoping to meet his mother all his life and enjoys every minute with her.'

'That's wonderful.'

'Yes, and I really like Michael.' Another blank silence.

'Mmm, well, it all sounds like great fun. Anything else?'

'Well...' Peter seemed to be struggling.

'Is there something in particular you wanted to ask me?' Carol could feel sleep seducing her as the silence stretched. 'Just say it.' Her eyelids were like lead.

'Okay.' He took a deep breath and out it came. 'Why did Dad leave Mum?'

Her eyes snapped open. 'You rang me from half way across the world to ask me *that*?'

'Sorry.' His voice was low and broken.

Carol sighed. This was a period in her childhood she had tried to forget, and it had been a family taboo forever. 'Don't be sorry. He left us too – and it wasn't our fault.' Was she reassuring her brother or herself? 'So, don't be sorry.' Her breath caught in her throat making it difficult to swallow. There was silence at the other end of the line. 'Are you still there?'

'Yeah,' softly, across the world.

'Look. I don't really know. I just remember the fights. They used to wait until they thought we were asleep and then it would start.' Like a bad smell the memory of her parents screaming came, as through a door ajar. Peter had unlocked that portal and the memories were flooding back. 'Sometimes it was about money. Sometimes it was about his drinking. And sometimes it was about other stuff that I didn't understand at the time. But I think it might have been about sex.'

'Oh,' said Peter, you never thought about your parents having sex – probably just as well. But somewhere at the back of his memory there were shrieking voices making him feel – unhappy maybe – and uncertain – and like the house was going to fall around his small, shaking body.

'Basically, I think he left because they were tearing each other apart. I remember him coming into my room one night and kissing me and saying goodbye. He never came back. But I didn't know it was the last time, so I pretended to be asleep. I've always wished I'd opened my eyes and put my arms around his neck.' Peter knew they had never heard from him again. He had tried to find his dad before his mother died and had met brick walls all the way.

'Do you and Gary fight?' Peter asked

Carol blotted her soggy eyes and took a deep breath, 'Sometimes. But then we make up. We both came from single parent families and think it's important to stay together – so we make sure we make up.' A watery smile appeared; sometimes making up was the best bit. 'Why are you asking me all this stuff?'

'Oh… well … when we were in a town yesterday there was a wedding in the main square. The Six Sisters crashed it.' He laughed. 'It was so beautiful. I mean, we didn't know the people, but they were in traditional dress and that seemed to make their day a part of long history. And then it was Kim and Tam's wedding anniversary and we all celebrated. It got me thinking about marriage and wondering why our family fell apart.'

'Our family *did not* fall apart. Our dad left but Mum held us all together. We were always a family – and we still are.' Big sister was back. 'And if you're worrying that people can't stay together – let me tell you it's possible. You just have to work on it.'

'That's what Elizabeth said.'

'Who's Elizabeth again?'

'The yes-woman.'

'Ah, well, she would.'

'Why?'

'Isn't she the one goes to church? Of course, she believes in marriage.'

'Oh.' This had never occurred to him.

'Is that all?' Carol thought that "all" in no way encompassed the rocky river of shared memory they had navigated. She wondered whether she would ever sleep again.

'No, I think that's about it.'

'Not planning to propose to anybody over there?'

'Definitely not.' She could hear Peter smiling into the phone.

'Stay safe, little brother. Don't do anything I wouldn't do.'

'Not even that,' replied Peter hearing the echo of his mother's words – that was her expression – as was his answer.

CHAPTER SEVENTEEN

From: Elizabeth
To: Katy
Subject: Day 7

Nuremberg is an amazing place with such a long and troubled history. You know I pray and today I found myself arguing with God quite a bit.

Some of us chose the WWII option today which began with a visit to the stadium where the Hitler rallies were held. I remember seeing film footage of this with thousands of young people lined up, their arms stiff from their shoulders like tank traps. Dilapidated and desolate, it is rotting quietly away as, no doubt, in foreign fields, are the bones of the beautiful young people who once filled this place with their zeal.

We went on then, in steadily increasing rain, dashing from the coach into Court Room

600 where the trials were held. Such a plain room to judge such atrocities. These men and women who thought they were gods, and held the sanctity of life so cheap, found their judgement here. Still, it is a sobering thought that ordinary folk can get carried along by the political flood and wreak such evil.

Sorry Katy, it is just so disturbing. Anna told us it would upset her too much. She had known people caught up in the Nazi movement and also young men conscripted from Vienna. Too many mixed feelings, she said. She and Kathryn chose the tour of the old town, Kathryn humming Wagner's Die Meistersinger's, the opera that was set here. They said the tour was beautiful and we all finished our visit together with gingerbread and coffee in the old town and a walk around the main square.

Last night we were entertained by a Bavarian group in dirndl and lederhosen – yodelling all the way.

~ ELIZABETH ~

I am struck down by this place. Laying here listening to Patsy quietly snore flat on her back, I am considering justice and judgement and forgiveness: the rights and wrongs of war.

The stadium was full of ghosts for me, as if they were my sons and daughters, whispering their betrayal. Were we not doing as our superiors told us? *say those beautiful Aryan boys,* Does God punish those who are obedient even unto death? *And the photos in the court room have the same puzzled expressions – why should judgement fall on us, they ask, we were only following orders.*

Is killing ever right? John would say no, and yet, if we are defending our nation, it is allowed. But who will defend the defenceless? I just know God is good and He brings relief for those afflicted. Seeing all this has made me grateful for a peaceful life where John never had to kill to defend me.

Elizabeth was alone in the lounge when Peter sat beside her. She looked weary, he thought, and a little melancholy.

'Are you okay?' he asked.

She nodded. 'Yes, I'm fine.'

'It's just… you look a little,' he was struggling for the right word, '… mmm… sad.'

She smiled at him and instantly his heart lifted. 'No, no,' she leaned forward and patted him on the hand. 'I was thinking about our day in Nuremberg. I just wrote to Katy about it and sent some photos. Such a sad history.'

Peter had been on the same tour as her and the frozen feeling of the courtroom sat like a millstone in his belly. He shook his head. 'It's unimaginable that ordinary people could be sucked into something like the Nazis.'

'I think it's too easy. Little by little, one law at a time. You just need to have a convincing end and any means becomes justifiable.'

'Could it happen to us, do you think?'

'It's always possible. We have to pray to God that we're never put in that position.' She added, 'And be careful who we vote for.'

Her talk of praying and God stirred up what Carol had said to him the night before. 'Do you?' he said.

'Do I what?'

'Pray to God.'

'Of course, I do,' she smiled at him, 'and I pray for you all the time... and Katy – and Bob – and all the Travel Club – and Justin – Justin needs lots of prayers.' They both laughed at this.

'Can I ask you something?' Peter was looking past her, over her shoulder, to the pewter river and its never-ending business of barges.

'Sure.'

'What do you think about marriage?'

Elizabeth had to consider this. Her grey curly head swivelled from side to side as if she was weighing it up. It had come out of left field and she wanted to make sure she gave a good answer. 'I think... I think... it's a blessing... but you have to take it seriously.'

He turned his head and looked at her face with its mix of gravity and grief.

She collected herself and went on, her eyes alight, 'For me it was my beginning and my end – and everything in between. Since I've been a... widow... I've realised how wonderful it was to be loved and love in return.' She shut her eyes and sighed, lost in her lost world. 'And I miss it.'

The last rays of sun flooded over them as they both weighed her words: other loves pervading their thoughts.

He launched in, 'Can I ask you something else?'

She nodded.

'Why get married in the first place? What if you change your mind?' He paused and thought as she watched him closely. 'What if you fall out of love – or the other person does?'

'That's three questions – well, four, really. Let me try to answer them as best I can. John and I got married because we wanted to spend our lives together and we had a wedding to tell everybody that we were promising before God to do that. I know it's different these days, but commitment and integrity go a long way in relationships.' His eyes were boring into hers. 'What if you change your mind?' She shrugged. 'Some people do and it's very sad. If you work on your marriage, and get help when you need it, I think it's less likely. You need to put each other first and be kind. The same goes for falling out of love. Most older couples will tell you that love changes from the first infatuation to something deeper and more knowing and grows with you through the seasons of life – if you tend and nurture it.'

'What about Bob? A kinder, more committed man, you couldn't find, and he thought everything was okay. Look what happened to him.' Peter crossed his arms, remembered Katy had told him that was body language for insecurity, and uncrossed them.

'Yes. That's very true. You try for honesty but never really know what's in another person's head.' The silence stretched taut as a slingshot, neither wanting to hurl a platitude into the discussion. Elizabeth relented. 'But that's just one marriage. What about Kim and Tam? What about Patsy – we all know the full details of her marriage.' She winked at him and he laughed. 'And John and I had lots of ups and downs, but we had a lifetime of love. Sometimes you have to step out in faith. And pray. I believe in that.' Elizabeth took a deep breath. 'It's champagne o'clock, how about I get us both a glass and you can tell me what's really on your mind.'

Peter felt his stomach sink as he watched her weave her way over to the bar, smiling at other passengers and responding to them as they greeted her. He was pondering whether he'd spill his guts.

The yes-woman sat in silence, waiting, sipping, bubbles flying up her nostrils as Peter finally said, 'I'm in love with Katy.'

She nodded. 'And how does Katy feel about it?' she asked, although she already knew the answer.

'The same, I think.' He pursed his lips. 'The thing is, I'm wondering if I'm too old for her… and too ordinary.' He sighed.

Elizabeth wagged her head from side to side, there was his mother's car dog again. 'I don't think she's the sort to start something if she thinks the other person is…' she searched for the word, 'inappropriate.'

'No.' He didn't think so either. Katy always had opinions. 'The thing is – I don't want an affair. I don't want just a girlfriend. I don't want to make her unhappy. I don't want her to finish with me and go off with somebody else. Lots of don'ts there, but what I really want is to spend the rest of my life with her. And,' and this was the big one, 'I don't know if I'm good husband material.'

Unbidden tears filled Elizabeth's eyes. 'Oh, Peter,' she said, her heart squeezed tight as she leaned forward and grasped his long-fingered hand, 'you are a wonderful, caring, kind – and handsome I might add – young man. You are perfect husband material. Have faith and ask her – that's all you can do – and see what she says.'

Peter was looking away again, over her shoulder, at the silvery river sliding past in the sunset. He jumped as somebody plonked down on a nearby chair.

'This looks serious,' said Di. 'What are you two talking about?'

'Nuremberg,' answered Elizabeth – a half truth, she thought, adding, 'and life.'

Peter's eyes slid back to her and she was nodding slightly. 'Yeah,' he said, 'important stuff.'

Di chugged back her champagne. 'Terrific history. I just loved that court room. So many stories there. Want another drink?' She rose, holding out her hands for their empty glasses.

'Yes, please,' they chorused.

CHAPTER EIGHTEEN

From: Patsy
To: Katy
Subject: Day 8

This morning we started with a long walk into Regensburg – longer because the boat still had one more lock to go. Anna and Kathryn stayed back on the boat and just as well as our guide moved like greased lightning as Ray would have said.

As we came over the bridge into town we noticed the pointed bases of the piers which are there to break the winter ice as it flows down the river. This is so far out of our experience. Australian rivers are lucky to have enough water to flow, let alone have ice in them. The town is a medieval masterpiece; its narrow alleys lead to chic shops, a Roman gate and wall, restful courtyards and churches redolent with community memories.

I was particularly enchanted with the huge painting of David and Goliath on one of the *buildings which represented the town standing up to the king of the time. Of course, it did not last as subsequent kings took the town. Various political leaders have contested for the power because of its place on the river. Still one Goliath victory is better than none.*

We walked for three hours until my legs were screaming. It was great to have a sitting afternoon, stepping down the Danube, passing farms and villages behind high, built-up river walls for flood mitigation.

We had our third session this afternoon and Kim and Di talked about travelling in the Orient. Rather bizarre for this setting, but the Travel Company wants us to cover as much as we can. It feels comfortable now to present our memories. A cup of tea in hand and we pretend we are with you, travelling in our imaginations. Di has done a fantastic job putting our old photos into video presentations. We just stop them every so often and tell stories. Then we get stories back from our audience – who are becoming friends. Then the guide shows some. Nothing too scary really.

The waves of emotion that washed over him had left Peter slightly unnerved. Visions of his own growing up years flickered like old movies through his days and hunted through his dreams. To sleep? He thought. His brain was running too fast, jerking him back and forth like an old red rattler. Instead he checked into his social media page and found Katy there.

PETER: *Hello. How are you going?*
That sounded a bit cliché.
KATY: *Do you know what time it is here?*
PETER: *You're the one that's still awake.*
KATY: *Well, I couldn't sleep.*
PETER: *Problems?*

Oh no, running the agency while he swanned about overseas might be too much for her. And did he really want to know about problems impossible to handle from half a world away?

KATY: *Not exactly. Hey, can we face time?*
PETER: *Sure.*

He hit the call button on the screen…

And there she was.

She was sitting up in bed in her pyjamas. Sans make-up, sans rings, sans hairdo. She looked gorgeous – and young, delectable, desirable, and… tired.

'What?' she said into the screen, and he realised all she could see was his mouth hanging open.

'Nothing.' He repositioned the screen, so she got his whole face. 'It's just lovely to actually see you.'

'Oh – well. Not at my best but here I am.' She waggled her head comically. 'At your service.' That sounded exciting, he thought. But she added 'Your local travel agent.'

Back to business, he realised. 'So, how's the agency going? Are you okay?'

'It's going fine. And, yes, I'm OK. I've just been having trouble sleeping. At night I think about all the things I need to do tomorrow – and the next day – and the day after that.' She didn't add that he haunted her dreams – day and night.

'You must have a list,' he said before he realised that the comic approach might be misinterpreted.

She smiled though. 'I do, but it gets longer and longer. Did you know Di's been sending snippets of the trip to the magazine and they've been putting them up on their social media? They have squillions of followers, so we've been getting heaps of enquiries about all sorts of destinations.' She sighed. 'I'm going to need a holiday after this.'

'Of course, you are. We can schedule it in when I get home.' He swallowed. 'How much time do you want to take?'

'Actually, I don't think I do. I certainly don't want to have a holiday on my own. It might just mean we're sharing the work again.'

'You could go away with your dad.'

'No, silly, I want to go with you.'

'Oh.'

She rushed on. 'And, of course, that's impossible because who would run the agency?'

'Oh,' he repeated, struggling with so many competing desires his brain buzzed like a beehive.

She looked intently at the screen and commented, 'You did say you missed me.'

The bees were settling, lining up, ready for the honey. He knew the answer to this. 'I do.'

'Well then…'

'Well then,' he smiled close to the screen, 'we will certainly have a holiday together when we can organise it at the same time. And,' he added before she could comment, 'if you need some R and R when I get home, you should also take some time off. Now tell me what's troubling you.'

Katy proceeded to list the issues she was facing at present with the solutions she had decided upon. Some things she had tackled before, and other challenges were new, and she had managed to work out her own ways to sort them out. Peter was impressed – and he told her so. He was surprised that a person who appeared so confident could need such reassurance – perhaps everybody did.

'So, now you've heard all my problems, tell me yours,' she said.

'I don't really have any problems,' he confessed and heard her groan. 'The women are going well – all enjoying the holiday and each other's company. The talk sessions are very well received. The cruise is terrific – great food, good company, and fantastic experiences. You couldn't wish for anything more.'

'That's wonderful,' she smiled tightly at him, trying not to grind her teeth.

'Except I do,' he said.

'Do what?'

'Wish for more.'

'More?' What on earth was he talking about…

'I wish for you.'

'Oh.'

Even on the fuzzy computer screen, he could see the pink rising up her cheeks.

'I miss you so much. I wish you were here.'

'You could send me a postcard.'

He laughed. 'Am I a cliché?'

She sighed. 'No, but I think I need to go to sleep if I'm getting up in three hours.'

'I'm sorry,' he said, 'I didn't mean to keep you up.'

'Yes, you did.' But she laughed. 'I'll be okay. I can always take a nap on the photocopier.'

'You could press the start button and send me a picture of it.'

'Like when Justin sat on it and photocopied his butt?'

That made them both laugh, and Peter was sitting transfixed with the notion of a picture of her bottom flying across the world to him. Before he could comment, she said, 'Good night', kissed the screen, and hung up.

CHAPTER NINETEEN

From: Kathryn
To: Katy
Subject: Day 9

Today I stood in Mozart's house – it was rhapsodic – I can't wait to tell my music students.

The visit Salzburg turned out to be a very long day, driving across Austria from Passau on the River up to the foothills of the Alps, with lots of castles, Romanesque churches and monasteries.

Salz refers to the salt mines nearby, which were active in Celtic and Roman times, and also during the Austro-Hungarian empire. It was made famous by the movie The Sound of Music. We visited the gardens where they filmed Do Re Mi – so I led our group in singing the song – and some jumped down the stairs as the children did in the movie. I have too much respect for my artificial hip to leap about on staircases.

We walked for two hours up through the Abbey and down through the town. Afterwards we could have coffee and wander about and my absolute dream came true. I visited the house where Mozart was born, which is now a museum. There were costumes, paintings, original manuscripts, his fortepiano – well a copy of it – and all sorts of wonderful things to drool over. I bet you didn't think I could drool – but this made me. The upper apartment where the Mozart family lived was reached by a very narrow staircase. One can only imagine how the women got up and down in their wide panier skirts. I imagined them turning sideways and sidling up and down like crabs. There are no photos because they were not allowed. I asked if they had a book about the museum, but they did not. There was nothing I could bring back. And for me the memories are wonderful – but I wish I could share them with you – and my students.

We came back to Linz via the Lake District which has a photo opportunity around every corner of the winding hilly roads. Delightful villages clustered around medieval churches, inviting turquoise lakes, golden flowered *meadows on deep green undulating hills. We visited the church where Maria married her Baron von Trapp in the movie and it was gilded with late sunshine. I could hear on the edge of my memory the anthem as Maria walked up the aisle towards the rainbow light from the tall windows. We arrived back exhausted and replete with the sound of music – one way or another.*

~ KATHRYN ~

I stood in Mozart's house. I walked around where his feet had trod as he conceived his wondrous music. I studied manuscript books full of his early works. I cannot believe it. The little blue book of simple Mozart music, that has been my constant conduit for transmitting the love of his music to beginners, was written there – where I stood – and I drew breath filled with so much joy.

When you give your life over to a passion like music, and the passing on of that passion, there are moments of rapture – and this was one. Can you be intimate with a long-dead composer? I have felt so. Studying, performing and teaching his music gives you a closeness, an understanding, an intimacy – I would say. It is as if the composer ripped out his insides and poured them into the ether – just for you. I love Mozart as he loved all of us – his audience.

The tears came rolling down as I studied the original manuscripts – my fingers itching to play them on the fortepiano. How sad there were no pictures I could bring home. I just have my memories of what I saw and heard – and the deep warm satisfaction in my gut.

Katy's dad, Bill, tapped her on the shoulder as she was rinsing the dinner dishes and she shot up so high he thought her head was going through the ceiling.

'What is *wrong* with you?' he asked, turning her around from the sink, propelling her across the room, and gently pushing her into his favourite armchair.

'I'm fine.' She tried to get up as he wiped her wet hands with a towel.

'No, you're not. You're mooning 'round the house. Hardly get a rise out of you anymore. Working all hours of the day and night. And… you haven't dyed your hair for ages… I can see your original colour coming back.' He ran a stubby finger down the middle of her mop to expose the two tones like nineteen forties' shoes. 'So,' he sat down opposite her, engulfing her damp hands in his to hold her down, 'Why don't you tell your old man what's wrong?'

Katy began to sniff and realised that tears were trickling down her cheeks and her nose was dribbling in sympathy.

Bill freed one hand, took out a crumpled hankie from his pocket and mopped her up. 'Long while since I've had to use the family hankie,' he said and smiled at her.

The memory twisted her gut — she was five and her mother was pulling the handkerchief out of her father's pocket to wipe her nose. Mum had always called it the family hankie. 'Oh, dad,' she whispered, 'I think I'm in love.'

No surprise there, he thought. 'Is it that travel agent fella?' He resumed his mopping. He had been watching them carefully at the lunch at Kim and Tam's and was convinced there was something going on. They were so careful — but they couldn't take their eyes off each other.

Katy nodded as the flood continued.

'Is it serious?' he continued, and her head bobbed up and down even more emphatically, trembling tears dropping like crushed crystals.

'Is it moving-in-together serious?' He knew kids did this now, he knew, marriage seemed old-fashioned.

She shrugged her shoulders.

'Do you want to do that?' he asked.

'I don't think so.' She shook her head. 'And he hasn't asked me.'

'Are you wanting to marry him?'

'He hasn't asked me that either.'

'Do you think he wants to?'

'I hope so.' There it was – out in the open. Suddenly, she knew what she wanted – to spend the rest of her life with Peter. Could Peter ever get the nerve up to ask her, even if he wanted to? 'He gets a bit nervous about things,' she muttered.

'You're a modern woman, you could ask him.'

She shook her head.

'He'd better do right by you or I'll go 'round and break his kneecaps.'

Katy laughed. 'You can't. He's in Europe.'

'Well… I'll meet him at the airport.' He wanted to ask how old was the fella? Was he really single? Had they actually slept together? She was, after all, a grown-up. He took a deep breath, swallowed his suspicions and exhaled trust, 'Whatever you want, I'm behind you.'

'Thanks Dad. But what if it means leaving you?'

'I'll cope,' he said. 'Just show me how to use the washing machine and the microwave and it'll all be hunky dory.' He looked at her again, registering her weariness. 'That's one thing. What about this tiredness. Are you sick?' Katy's mother had been continually tired before they realised how ill she was. He had watched his daughter surreptitiously over the years for any signs that she also might have a dicky heart.

'It's just work, Dad. The agency is absolutely crazy at present and I don't know whether we can afford to hire anybody else. I don't want to worry Peter with it, but Bob and I are barely coping.'

'You need to do something. He won't be happy to come home to a scarecrow.'

She rolled her eyes at him.

'And don't you roll your eyes at me, young lady, go and look at yourself in the mirror.'

The Travel Club

She had and really didn't want to repeat the experience.

'What do you need?' he asked.

'Well, I suppose we could do with another travel agent, but I don't have the authority to hire anybody like that. Even a temp who could answer the phone and run errands for us would be a huge help. That's what Bob used to do but now he's doing Peter's job.'

There was silence as they both turned the issue over in their minds.

Finally, Bill spoke, 'How about I come in and be your dogsbody. I can answer phones and do whatever you want me to do. And, if I don't know how to do something, you can teach me. I'm a quick learner. Don't pay me much. Since I'm on a pension, I can only earn a little bit. I'll be there whenever you need me.' He was watching her face as she sifted through the pros and cons. 'You don't have to have me if you don't want to,' he added.

'Actually,' replied Katy, 'that would be great.' She had been anxious about him since his retirement; constantly at home, glued to the TV, living his life through a flickering screen. This would give him purpose and help her at the same time – she hoped. 'How about you come in from ten to three through the week and full time on Saturdays when we're really busy – just until Peter's back again. Can you start tomorrow?'

He nodded, then smiled. 'Fancy working for my little daughter.'

She swallowed the surge of apprehension and grinned back. 'It'll be great.' Who was she assuring, she wondered, her father or herself?

He pulled her up out of the armchair and pushed her towards the bathroom. 'Go and dye your hair. I like it bright.'

CHAPTER TWENTY

From: Di
To: Katy
Subject: Day 10

Today we visited Melk with its amazing library. The smell is incredible. It has been a place for production of manuscripts since medieval times and there are still some in the library. All those books – all those words – all those thoughts preserved for all time. Centuries of thoughts have their own peculiar fragrance – dry velum, old paper, like pressed flowers – but still affecting and worthy and meaningful. They hold knowledge and power, yearning and achievement, passion and persistence. This place really spoke to my soul. I imagined a long line of writers going back more than a millennium, struggling with their creations, not giving up, leading to me.

The town nestles on the river and high up on the overlooking hill is the enormous

Benedictine Abbey built in High Baroque style in the 18thC. Kings and queens used this mansion? Palace? Castle? Abbey? I guess – as a motel and there are endless paintings of the Austro-Hungarian royal family frequenting this hostelry. Throughout there were ceilings that were painted to look as if they were curved – all of them clever optical illusions known as trompe l'oeil. We filed past displays of the gold robes the abbot wore. There is so much gold in all the churches and abbeys on this tour – makes you wonder where they got it all from. Maybe the river traders made rich by their constant traffic when the new world gave up its riches. That would be interesting to write about.

Following our visit to the Abbey we wandered back down through the town, past quaint houses and shopping opportunities – even I am becoming an accomplished shopper with all this training. Lol. Then our vessel sailed on down the Danube through the much-castellated and vinyarded Wachau Valley to Durnstein. Here we had a wine tasting and welcome sleep, helped along by the morning's hike and the Gruner Weitliner wine that is produced in this area. Anna was standing next to me at the vineyard and as she tasted the wine, her eyes opened wide and there was ripple of recognition across her body. She sipped again and held my elbow to steady herself, 'I remember,' she said, and I raised my eyebrows, 'Remember?', 'the taste – it makes me remember.' And she closed her eyes to savour the rest of the glass and all it recalled.

In the afternoon the Open Travel Club had its last public session and we all had a chance to have our say. Elizabeth spoke about the remembered joy of her post-retirement trip with John. Patsy's topic was travelling in Egypt – do you know she flew out five days before the Arab Spring revolution? Now that is fascinating. Kim talked about her life in Vietnam before it became communist. Tam sat quietly nodding his encouragement and smiling at her, even when both their eyes were full of tears. Anna talked about growing up in Vienna and attending the Conservatorium there. Kathryn spoke about Mozart – since we are in his land. And me – I talked about how much The Travel Club mattered to me – and how it had changed my life. Peter wound it all up and – surprisingly for all of us – told everybody about his mother: how he had looked after her and missed her every day – and then he said he couldn't bring his mum – but he was delighted to be here with his Travel Mums. Of course, I would be more like his big sister, but I get it. And it was beautiful.

After dinner we were entertained by a group from Salzburg. Kathryn was ecstatic as they sang Mozart Ariettas and the rest of us really enjoyed the numbers from the Sound of Music. Anna's eyes were mostly closed. Still savouring, I guess.

From: Di
To: Bob
Subject: Our Wish List

Dear Bob

Let's put Melk on our wish list. You would love it. So ornate – and Baroque – and over the top. I so wish you had been there to see it with me. My writing is going well, and the Abbey has really encouraged me – in an odd sort of way (all those books redolent with ideas) – to keep on with it. I plan to ring you tonight. xx

~ ANNA ~

We are drifting down this beautiful Blue Danube and I am drifting in and out of streams of memory. They shift around me, in and out of time and place so that I can scarcely recognise where I am or who I am.

I have stepped into the poster on the travel agent's window and I am the child dangling her feet over the edge into the water. I am the girl waving her blue-ribboned hat to the bargeman. I am the mother holding the child back with the leading strings.

The river flows around me – and through me. It is gushing through my veins, rushing around my heart, crushing the walls I have built around my life. The combed hills of vineyards are my sinews; the castles and medieval towns, my bones;

the people that populate them, my heartstrings – I recognise my face in theirs'.

I have served my exile. Is it now my time to come home? Do you know vein is so like Vien – my place. The love of this place is coursing through my veins. Is it only nostalgia or is the world twisting?

For so long I was the reffo, the new-Australian, the alien. Australian and Austrian are so close, just two letters away, yet I was always the outsider. I left behind all that was me and embraced a new Anna. Can the new Anna bring the old Anna home?


```
From: Peter
To: Katy
Subject: wish you were here
```

The sisters are so overwhelmed they asked me to write to you about what happened.

Heading towards Vienna, we sailed down the beautiful Danube surrounded by blue sky, blue water, bright green vineyards and half-timbered villages flowing into towns. The warmth of the day had lured everybody out on deck to soak up the sun. The mooring place was a few kilometres from the city, so we were surprised to see a crowd on the wharf where we were to dock – maybe a beer festival like in Bamberg, Di suggested.

There were people of all ages. They were dressed in dirndls and lederhosen and all chattering to each other. As our river ship approached the pier they raised their arms and waved enthusiastically. The sisters and I were on the top deck and Patsy joked, 'Oh, look, they knew we were coming – it's a welcome party.' Everybody laughed. And then, as we docked, the captain and Michael appeared and took Anna by each elbow, gently walked her down the stairs to the gang plank and across to the dock. A young man with a violin came out from the crowd playing Strauss' Vienna Woods. Anna began to sing along, her voice cracking, snatches of her song coming to us on the upper deck. She was moving slowly towards the violinist and the semicircle of people behind him. An announcement came over the boat's loudspeaker asking everybody else to stay on board for the moment and enjoy the welcome for one of their very special passengers. This was her family, the disembodied voice told us, who had been waiting a lifetime to meet her.

Michael moved from his mother's side and embraced an elegant middle-aged woman, his wife we found out later, and then presented her to Anna. I could see Anna shaking and smiling and laughing and sobbing. And I had a sudden flash of her standing outside the agency, drab and down, almost two dimensional as she gazed at the Vienna poster. And here she was, transfigured into more dimensions than I could number.

Shuffling slowly around the semi-circle, Anna was introduced to Michael's children and grandchildren. Each child gave Anna a flower, then a kiss as she embraced them. Michael's wife kept handing Anna tissues to soak the tears that coursed down her face.

She was glancing over her shoulder at the young man with the violin and when she reached the end of the semicircle, he walked towards her, finished the music and put his arms around her, the violin dangling down behind her stooped back. 'Grandmother,' he said, 'Come with me,' and took her over to a group of elderly people smiling tentatively at her. 'We think we have found some friends of yours.' They were all shaking hands with Anna and kissing her on both cheeks and one lady in a scarf covered in roses came forward and Anna and she clung together, weeping on each other's shoulders, the roses covering them both like a wreath.

By now all the sisters were weeping – and I admit my nose was dripping. The captain came to us and said, 'How do you like the welcome?' The women all sobbed their thanks and he magically produced a box of tissues and handed it around. 'Her family could not wait,' he told us, 'They contacted the company and asked could they meet her as soon as we landed in Vienna.'

More crying – I thought they were going to sink the boat with all the water on the deck. Then he ushered the Travel Club down out onto the dock and we were also greeted by the family. They kept saying how pleased they were to see us. And thanking us for making their dear mother and grandmother's dream come true. My hand was wrung so much my wrist is still aching. Before we knew it, the whole boatload of passengers was out on the dock joining the festivities and the staff were passing around champagne and orange juice.

The captain stood at the head of the gang plank resplendent in his white uniform and called for quiet. 'A toast,' he said, 'to Anna.'

'To Anna,' replied the crowd as one, raising their glasses.

Michael emerged from the congregation and stood beside the captain, raising his glass, 'To my darling mother – who was lost – and now is found.'

My Darling Katy – so many times on this trip I have wished you were with me. But today I would have given anything to have you stand beside me there with Anna's family. For me to say to them that you, Katy, are the reason they have found Anna. You are the one who made these wonderful women part of our world.

Jeanie Wood

From: Elizabeth
To: Katy
Subject: Day 11

Hi Katy

What a day we've had. After the party Anna and her family went to one of their houses and had a great big catch up. The rest of us, and indeed all the passengers went off on a tour of Vienna. Kathryn LOVED the statue of Mozart in the Burggaten near the Hofburg Palace. Patsy loved the Schonbrunn Palace with its orangerie and beautiful gardens. I loved St Stephen's Cathedral and the main square. Kim and Tam loved drinking coffee and eating apple strudel in the main street. You can see we've played what was your favourite part of the day – of course for everybody, it was Anna's coming home and after that we found these other things to love as well. The sun continued to shine on us and there was a lot of happiness going around after our morning lesson in loving.

Tonight, Anna and Michael joined the rest of us for a delightful concert at the magnificent Palace Lichtenstein – with more gold on the walls than you could poke a stick at – and that includes the conductor with his baton. We all fell into our beds, absolutely spent.

On the top deck, soaking up the mid-morning sunshine, Peter and Michael were enjoying a local beer.

'How's your mother?' asked Peter, leaning back in his favourite seat, sunglasses turned heavenward.

'Exhausted. She's staying in bed this morning. Kathryn's caring for her. This afternoon my wife and I are taking her on a little tour. We plan to go to the place where she grew up and the Conservatorium where she met my father.'

'Good thing she's resting then.' They looked out over the green shoreline and the people going about their everyday business.

'When we reach Budapest, she and Kathryn will travel with us to our home in the hills for a week,' said Michael, 'Then the family can come and visit in little groups and get to know her better. Afterward my wife and I are booked to accompany my mother and her friend back to Australia and stay for a while.'

Peter nodded. He and Katy had planned the post-tour arrangements. Kim and Tam were off to London to their daughter. Anna and Kathryn staying on with Michael. And Peter would accompany Elizabeth, Patsy, and Di for a three-day extension in Paris before they flew home. Lord knows how that would go! He wished he could dump Paris and fly straight back into Katy's arms.

'You have a wonderful family,' he said to Michael.

'We're very lucky,' agreed Michael.

'How did you meet your wife?' Peter still had marriage on his mind and the morning beer was loosening his tongue.

'Actually, I met her at church. We were teenagers when her family returned to live in our village and we became instant friends. Soul mates, I think you call it.'

'How did you know your marriage would last?' Like a dog with a bone, Peter thought the yes-woman might say if she heard his question.

'We didn't,' Michael was shaking his head, 'I mean, we wanted to spend our lives together – but there is no assurance. Just hard work and prayer.' He laughed. 'And my wife would tell you more hard work and prayer on her part than mine. But after all these years, we love each other dearly.'

'Do you still go to church?'

'Yes, we do. We both still practise our faith. We believe God has kept us together all these years, been with us in the hard times – and we've had those – and given us much happiness.' He sipped his beer. 'And now He has given me back my mother.'

Confession was good for the soul, Peter had heard, maybe it was time. 'I've been thinking a bit about marriage lately.' He looked up to see Michael observing him. 'And a bit about God too.'

Michael pursed his lips. 'Is there a reason?'

'Yes.' Peter was collecting his thoughts. Honesty seemed best. 'Yes, there is. I'm in love with a girl at home and I want a proper relationship. She's a bit old-fashioned and I find I want to be old-fashioned too. I'm thinking about asking her to marry me,' then added, 'in a church – properly.'

'Do you go to a church?' Michael was trying to make sense of this.

'No,' Peter answered, 'but Elizabeth does. It's close to where we live. I thought we might get married in her church.'

Michael nodded. 'Why don't you go along and try it out first? See if it's okay. Take your girl, too.'

That sounded logical, Peter thought. 'I might just do that.' He took a deep breath, here was the nub of his problem. 'I'm also worried about being a good husband.' He rushed on, 'My dad left when I was small, so I don't really know what a husband – or father for that matter – is supposed to do.'

'Oh,' said Michael. He felt sorry for this earnest young man. 'Well, you just need to discuss things, and be kind and considerate, and take care of your wife.' He watched Peter nodding and thought some more. 'Why don't you ask Elizabeth if they have pre-wedding guidance at your church? That might help.'

Peter was looking at him like he came from Mars.

Michael had another thought. 'Have you asked her yet?'

Peter flashed him a forlorn face. 'No, no,' he stammered, 'I might do it when I get home.'

'Yes, you *must*,' Michael said bracingly, 'but try to hint at it before you actually propose. Then you can maybe work out how she feels about the whole thing.'

Peter's gut twisted tight in his belly. How she feels about it… he didn't even know how he felt about it. Or maybe he did. A new resolve flowed through his veins. 'Can I ask you a question?'

'Certainly.' Michael thought privately, Peter had already been asked quite a few questions, it was a bit late to be asking permission.

'Did you live together before you were married?'

'No,' said Michael, 'people did not so much in our day. We didn't even sleep together before we were married.'

Now Peter was taken aback. 'Really?'

'Really,' said Michael. 'We were both virgins when we were married – just kids, really. But we shared the same beliefs.'

'How did that work out?'

'Well, we weren't very good at it to start with, but we got better.' He laughed. 'Obviously – you've met our children.'

'So, it was okay for her too?'

'Still is.' Michael had a quiet grin on his face.

'Oh,' murmured Peter – too much information. He rallied, 'Maybe I need some guidance on that too.'

'There's some good books around – and web sites, as well.'

Michael had obviously conducted conversations like this before – well, he did have sons. 'I wish I'd had a dad like you.' Mouth in gear before brain, Peter thought, he hadn't meant to say it out loud.

'I could always adopt you,' said Michael, 'it worked for me.' He laughed – then shrugged, 'ask me anything you like. But for now,' he raised his stein, 'Skoll,' toasted Michael, 'and may the Force be with you.'

Head down, Peter guzzled his beer and thought he'd need more than a light sabre to build his empire.

```
From: Kim
To: Katy
Subject: Day 12
```

A new day and Tam and I took an optional tour to Bratislava in Slovakia. Driving through the suburbs of Vienna first then into rich farming lands and kilometres of greenhouses so that year-round people here enjoy fresh fruit and vegetables. Eventually we crossed the border into the former Soviet republic. This was very challenging for us. We are learning how to be tourists and practising not being scared at border crossings – particularly into former communist countries. Here, there are huge fields because private farms were socialised, and farmers were made to build the ugly concrete city to live in while they worked on communal fields. This made us very sad as these buildings replaced the original small farms that surrounded the medieval town.

The city has a castle which is fantastic on the outside but inside is just a shell, stripped bare of history. Lining the hill to the castle are the luxurious post-war villas for the communist party officials. This made us very angry – so much for equality. We walked through the old town starting with a barbican – which now I know is two gates at right angles to each other from the outer to the inner wall to catch invaders. This country seems to have always been occupied – Turks, Austro-Hungarians, Napoleon, Nazis and the Russians all ruled here. It has been a state of some great power, apart from a few years between the two world wars. The main streets are restored but the side ones have rundown buildings with graffiti and bullet holes. It has the feeling of recovering from a long sickness and still not back to full health.

The day was finished with the Captain's Farewell Cocktail party, during which we were once again introduced to the passengers who all applauded us. Wow. This was followed by a five-course dinner. Double Wow – in my grandson's words.

'I have something for you.' Peter rose from his chair with six tiny boxes. Each had a letter on top.

'E,' he said, 'for Elizabeth,' and presented it to her, 'don't unwrap it yet. I want you to open them all together.'

Around the dinner table he walked, handing out boxes with the correct letter to each of the women.

Having completed a full circle, he stood behind his own chair.

The women were holding their packages with the tips of their fingers, eyes sparkling. Michael, Tam, and the captain were gazing at him. There was no doubt a speech was in order, and Peter was gathering his thoughts and his courage as his knuckles turned white on the polished chairback.

'I've thought a lot about this,' he said, 'I really wanted you to have something to remember this time.'

There were murmurs of denial around the table – as if they could ever forget.

'I thought a lot about what I should give you. Maybe an old travel brochure each,' they all laughed, and he smiled, 'cheap – but heavy on the plane.' He shook his head. 'No. Don't open them yet. Then I thought a coffee or tea cup each – with a cake plate of course.'

They were laughing again.

'Better count the crockery,' Michael said to the captain.

Peter shook his head. 'Too hard to carry porcelain home.'

Laughing, Patsy looked sideways at Elizabeth, who was judiciously ignoring her and trying to control her face.

Peter caught the look, blinked, and shook his head, eyes narrowed. Back on task, he continued, 'I wanted to show you what you have given – and give you something to say thank you. Open them up and you'll see.'

Each box was unwrapped and opened. Inside there was a chain with a gold heart with T C woven in the filigree and a precious stone gleaming in the middle. The stones were slightly different colours that matched the women's outfits.

'I hope the colours are right.' He had asked Katy for advice but was a bit concerned by the women's silence and then realised it was tears suppressed, stopping words. Here goes, he thought, 'I wanted to give you each a heart because you have offered us yours.'

The tears were flowing freely. He leaned forward and picked up his glass of champagne. 'A toast,' he announced, 'to the Travel Club.

Who have offered their stories, their lives and their hearts to us – and,' he took a deep breath, 'filled ours with joy.'

He heard a shuffle of feet and chair legs as everybody in the dining room rose, raised their glasses and saluted: 'To the Travel Club, Thank you.' He heard behind him. 'Thank you,' he echoed.

As he sat, he heard Di's stage whisper from behind her camera to Elizabeth, 'Say something.'

The yes-woman, Peter thought, for the first time in history, was bereft of words. He watched her slowly clasp the chain around her neck and then wipe her eyes as she stood.

'What can I say to that?' She looked at Peter. 'He's a hard act to follow,' she smiled and turned to address the room. 'Let me try to thank you all. We…' she gestured towards the women around the table now wearing their hearts, 'we've had a wonderful time. It started in a local travel agency in a very ordinary shopping mall on the other side of the world. Well, not actually in it.' She laughed. 'Just outside it, drooling over these beautiful places in the posters. And here we are,' she swept her hands out, encompassing the table, 'we've become part of those pictures. It's like the first time we walked through those glass doors and met Peter, we stepped through the looking glass and found Wonderland.'

They all clapped, and she held up her hands to quieten them, 'but what I really want to say is thank you. Thank you for looking after us all. Thank you for this wonderful holiday. Thank you for our beautiful hearts. I know,' she smiled at the other women and corrected herself, '*we* know they come from your kind hearts which made all of this possible. So,' she raised her glass, 'here's to kindness and love – a magic bowl that refills even as you pour it out. And to our Peter, a kind patron, our sheep dog, and beloved travel son.'

The whole room raised their glasses. Peter discreetly blew his nose.

'Let's play the game again.' Dinner had been cleared and Di was wined up. 'What was your favourite part about the trip?'

'Tell us yours first,' answered Kathryn, giving the others time to think.

'I loved Melk – all those books in the library. Did you smell them?' She was waving her arms around and the others were nodding. 'Sorry, I just get excited about any books and old ones are totally thrilling. Who's next?'

'My turn,' Kathryn jumped in. 'I loved Mozart's house. To be in the place where he wrote all his early works. I still wish I could have played his forte piano. Totally mind blowing.'

Anna laughed. 'Yes, she was very emotional. Went on and on and on. No need to tell you what my favourite was. Of course, I loved everything, but, meeting my son and then his family – there are no words I can use to describe this. My heart has been taken apart and built back again – so it's new.' She ran out of breath and words simultaneously and nodded at Kim. 'Your turn,' she whispered.

'We had a lovely anniversary day and that night with all our travel family.' Kim looked to Tam, who nodded. 'It would be hard to say what we liked best. The whole holiday is a wonder for us that we never expected. It has been beautiful.'

There was silence at the table and Di turned to Patsy and Elizabeth. 'What about you two?'

'Amsterdam,' they chorused, laughed, and left it at that.

CHAPTER TWENTY-ONE

From: Patsy
To: Katy
Subject: Day 13

Today was our last full day on the boat in Budapest. We got up early for breakfast – in fact we were so early there was nobody in the dining room and we thought we had the wrong place hahaha. After that we sailed down the Danube between Buda and Pest looking at all the wonderful buildings. Wonderful must be the wrong word – I could try fantastic, or amazing, or, my favourite, gob-smacking. When we docked we had some spare time so some of us went walking and found the market – oh the beautiful embroidery, and the dolls – Elizabeth bought two of the dolls for granddaughters and I bought two for me. Why not. After lunch we had a coach tour of the town including the opera house where a troubadour entertained the group. Very romantic. We visited Castle Hill and St. Steven's church. Steven seems to be very popular in this part of the world – he built churches everywhere. On Castle Hill they have been digging and found medieval buildings under the ground. And inside the hill is an abandoned WWII hospital built there to be safe from the bombing.

Back at the ship we were treated to a Hungarian performance of dancers and violinists which was more Eastern European than previous entertainment. After dinner we had a glorious treat to end our journey – a trip down the river with all those gob-smacking buildings lit up like fairyland. Unbelievable – breath-taking – a superb finish to an unforgettable journey.

Thank you, Katy, for making this possible.

It was three o'clock on the Tuesday before Bill had the opportunity to go out for the lunches. 'I shouldn't be going,' he said to Katy, 'you should go and have a break. All you do is sit in front of that computer screen all day. You need to get out in the fresh air,' he said, completely ignoring the fact that they were in a mall.

'He's right,' Bob's voice came from behind another computer screen, 'have a break.'

'Peter left me the boss here – not you two Bs.' She had taken to calling them B1 and B2 – that left her as the Queen B, she imagined. 'Leave me alone and let me finish my work. All I need is a salad sandwich and a hot chocolate and I'll be fine.'

The Travel Club

'You're gunna to get sick if you keep this up,' said her dad, and Bob humphed in agreement.

She shook her head. 'Next week we'll all be back to normal and then I promise I'll have a proper lunch hour every day.'

'Humph.' Bill liked to express himself this way

'Humph,' echoed B1 who had picked it up like a head-cold from B2.

The truth was the agency was booming. Justin came in the afternoons as often as he could wangle it with his schoolwork – and his mum and dad – and looked after a lot of the information coming back from the Travel Club. He had even taken to going next door at the end of the day to admire Di's photos of the Six Sisters in the dress shop. A bit of female attention made him feel very adult. The shop assistants told him they had found a whole new market of older women who could imagine themselves in the clothes after they'd seen the Travel Club wearing them with spectacular holiday backgrounds.

It had become apparent to Justin that the ads of young people doing things – and wearing things for that matter – missed the market by quite a stretch. He had shared this with the three Bs the day before and even dared to add by which percentage he thought marketing both travel and clothing – and maybe lots of other things – were ignoring other generations. Katy looked unsurprised, she had been working on this strategy ever since the first client asked to talk to the Travel Club. Bill looked like Justin was teaching his grandmother to suck eggs – a favourite expression of his – of course he didn't buy stuff that young people liked – he pleased himself. Bob looked proud – that astonished Justin – that this young man was finding an opportunity to apply the maths he had so hated just a month or so ago.

But Justin was not coming today. There was only the three of them.

Bill came back with the lunches, put them on the Travel Club table and gestured to Bob to come over. He stomped back to Katy, pulled her new wheelie chair gently back and rolled her across the room. 'Take a break,' he said. The phone rang. He pushed her chair under the table firmly and answered the phone himself.

'Let me take a message, she's in a meeting right now, she'll get back to you as soon as possible,' he said into the phone, glaring at Katy the whole time as he wrote down the message.

'Am I allowed to go to the Ladies Room?' asked Katy when she had finished her lunch – deceptively obedient thought her father.

He nodded. 'And don't rush back.'

'We'll look after everything,' said B1 and B2 nodded

Wandering back through the mall, Katy decided her father and Bob were probably right. She stopped at the hairdressers and said hello, answering their questions about the travellers and noticing some new photos of Kathryn and Anna with their holiday hairdos.

At the butchers, she bought some meat for dinner and decided to get enough for three and ask Bob over. The two Bs had become good friends.

Finally, she walked into the clothing shop next door and was stunned at the poster displays of the Travel Club wearing their clothes on holidays. Kathryn and Anna were there standing with Michael in Vienna at the statue of Mozart surrounded by a rainbow of roses. Kim and Tam were caught crashing the wedding party in a medieval square, white doves rising like confetti on the breeze. Patsy and Elizabeth were poking around an Amsterdam cheese shop. Wow, she thought, they all look great and Di's photos are wonderful. Where was Peter in all this, she wondered, missing in action. And she was missing him.

'Do you have anything in my style?' she asked the assistants, not really knowing what her style was anymore.

'Is it for a special occasion?' asked the younger woman.

'Maybe. I'm not sure. It could be.' Katy was feeling less responsible by the minute. 'Show me what you've got,' she said, ignoring the incessant phone ringing in the shop next door.

The Travel Club

From: Elizabeth
To: Katy
Subject: Day 14

It was sad to say goodbye to Kathryn and Anna and Michael – of course I know they will have a wonderful time and we'll see them again soon.

Michael's wife brought their car down and picked them all up. We travelled to the airport with Kim and Tam and Peter saw them on the plane to London and ours left an hour later for Paris.

Our hotel is right next to the Seine and we can see the river from our bedroom window. The first place we went was the Eiffel Tower. It is very crowded and has high security but Peter had booked us in to go up and also have lunch there. The view was spectacular.

What a beautiful city it is – so neatly arranged like a town planner exercise. Apparently, this was because Napoleon knocked down medieval Paris and built his own. Maybe he was the first town planner. We walked down the Champs D' Elysees and then had a cruise along the Seine. The boat commentary was terrific with lots of local history. We sailed past the Louvre, Notre Dame and so many more historic buildings.

As night fell, Paris came alive and so did

> the Eiffel tower as it looked like gold
> filigree - like our beautiful heart
> necklaces. Suddenly there was a light show
> and it became a tower of diamonds, burning
> brighter than the stars.

Peter took a picture of the Eiffel Tower light show on his phone and sent it to Katy.

PETER: *Here's your postcard. Wish you were here.*

Ding!

KATY: *Me too*

PETER: *Not long now*

Ding!

KATY: *counting the days*

PETER: *Me too*

Ding!

KATY: *how's the weather?*

PETER: *Hot.*

Ding!

KATY: *like you*

PETER: *How would you like to come here for a holiday?*

Ding!

KATY: *yes please.*

PETER: *We will need to book it*

Ding!

KATY: *I'll ask a good travel agent*

PETER: *A romantic getaway?*

Ding!

KATY: *you're not getting away from me*

```
PETER: Good
```
Ding!
```
KATY: Goodnight xx
```

He smiled at his phone. Was that dipping his big toe in the water? He thought it might be. Time to go shopping.

CHAPTER TWENTY-TWO

From: Patsy
To: Katy
Subject: Day 15

Oo la la - we are in Paree. The Seine looks like glass today.

Setting off early in our walking shoes, we began with a climb to Montmartre, with its beautiful Sacre Couer. There were pilgrims in the cathedral from all over the world, dressed in jeans and T shirts with special scarves to show their pilgrimage. How wonderful to have such faith. In the square outside there is an artist's colony. Lots of beautiful paintings and crafts to buy. We bought Peter a special tie with a cat on it. I can feel my suitcase swelling - as are my feet.

On then down through the streets of Paris to the Louvre. Peter had also pre-booked this and so we had an easy entry compared to the lines of waiting tourists. We spent three hours here, but I could spend three months. All that art – mind you there are quite a few pictures of Napoleon.

We sat – that felt good – and had bread and cheese for lunch. Then we moved on to the Musee D'Orsay where all the artists from the mid-1800s to the post-impressionists are represented. I could definitely spend three years there – just sitting soaking up the paintings – imbibing the beauty. We strolled slowly back to the hotel and had dinner at a local café tonight.

I thought my feet were worn through, but we decided it would be a crime to waste a beautiful Paris evening. So, we had a little walk along the silvery Seine under the moon and stars. You would have loved it.

'So, what are you doing when we get home?' said Patsy.

'Sleeping,' answered Elizabeth.

'And after that?'

'Bringing Molly home.'

Patsy laughed. 'And feeding her up?'

Elizabeth rolled her eyes. 'Then – the first Monday back is Ladies Fellowship at church and they asked me to talk about my holiday. I have to organise that. I thought I might put some photos up and that would help me remember everything.'

'Can I come?'

Elizabeth tried not to look too surprised. 'Sure. You could help me talk about the trip. We can show them our souvenirs.'

'I could take my dolls.'

'The ladies would love them,' Elizabeth said.

'What about the souvenirs from Amsterdam?'

'Maybe not.' They chorused and laughed.

Patsy said, 'I've decided to try out church with you. I think it's time I found my faith again.'

'You'll be most welcome,' answered Elizabeth, sending up silent thanks.

```
From: Di
To: Katy
Subject: Day 16
```

Last day of the holiday and Peter booked us a visit to Versailles. What a big finish. It is absolutely magnificent with killer cobble stones, so our feet are very sore and are screaming *give us a rest*. Ah well, they can rest on the long flight home. You can see a lot of things have been changed at Versailles since Marie Antoinette ate cake there. Napoleon has a lot to answer for – there are many rooms he altered. Maybe he didn't like cake. Still there's lots to see. We went through the chambers of Louis XIV (Sun King), XV, XVI (beheaded) and also the Hall of Mirrors where they signed the treaty to end WW1. Then out in the gardens to watch the fountains playing to music by Rameau, the court composer for Louis XIV – Kathryn would have loved this. The whole day was one great photo opportunity stacked on top of another.

Yes, I took lots of pics. After our tour we were brought back to a shopping area, so we could support the French economy. This is our last diary email – our thoughts are turning towards home. I have had a lovely holiday and I am really glad I came but it will be good to be home, back in my own bed, and see you *all* again.

Peter was dreaming he'd mislaid something. Not sure what. He only had three women with him, so he really had lost three of the Travel Club. They were in a strange airport, with foreign notices everywhere. He was trying to communicate with sign language and the women were all talking at once in different languages. Katy was in the distance but no matter how far he walked, she moved further away. He cried out to her, but she was not looking at him. Somebody was pulling on his arm and he was suddenly awake.

'Are you okay?' whispered Di from the plane seat next to him. 'You yelled out.'

Rubbing his stubbly face, he nodded and switched on the screen – they were flying over inland Australia. Adelaide was marked, and Broken Hill, and it made his heart swell to think he was coming home. Dreams were strange things, he mused, not portents but more anxieties buried deep emerging when your mind relaxes. Michael had encouraged him to have faith in his relationship with Katy, and that's what he planned to do. He looked across the aisle at Patsy and Elizabeth. Both women were fast asleep, heads lolling, mouths gaping, snoring softly. He smiled and turned back to Di who was busy typing away on her small tablet.

'Have you slept at all?' he asked

'No, I can't get comfortable. I'll sleep when I get home.'

'Try not to sleep till dark.' Peter knew the hazards of jetlag and sleep patterns.

'I'll do my best.'

'How's the writing going?'

'It's going well. You've seen the small articles I've written?'

He nodded

'I have a larger one – that's what I'm committed to.' Di went on, 'But it's the photos that have really taken off. They tell such a story. I took some of passengers as well. Did you know that?'

This was news to Peter. 'No, I didn't.'

'The cruise director liked what I was doing and asked me to extend my collection. I may get an invitation to take photos and write about another cruise.'

'Wow,' said Peter, 'how do you feel about that?'

'We'll see,' she replied, 'I'll have to talk to my agent about that.'

He raised his eyebrows.

'Bob,' she said, and he laughed.

'I'm sure he'll sort it out.' He said knowingly.

'Yes he will.' And she smiled widely and got back to her writing.

Airports, Elizabeth thought, the chicken soup of the world. You take some flying objects, empty them into an expanse, throw in every imaginable nation and stir. It looked like it was simmering away nicely. Passengers milled around the carousels, waiting for their baggage to pop up like vegetables in a stew pot. Customs officials with their busy little beagles weaving in and out of the mix. Aircrews slipping between spent travellers in Teflon streams. Nearly home, she thought, and was caught between joy and regret.

Weary and wordless, she and Patsy sat on a bench in the baggage hall as Peter, nobly assisted by Di, reclaimed their luggage. Why was she so tired when they had slept, she wondered, as the world floated around her? She felt disconnected – loose from her heavy body.

Peter suddenly appeared in front of her. 'Your bag seems to be missing.' His voice came from a long way and woke her. 'I'm going to see if I can find it.'

Off he went, and Di plopped down on the seat next to her, patting her on the arm and saying, 'I'm sure it'll be okay. He'll find it.'

Elizabeth just nodded and stared at the vacant carousel. She had plenty of clothes at home – why were they fussing?

Half an hour later, Peter came striding across the hall – bagless. 'I'm sorry,' he said, 'they can't find it. I have all the documents here – the airline will contact you as soon as they have it and get it to you.'

'That's all right.' She sighed. 'Better now than at the start of the trip. Let's go home.' They walked past customs – nothing to declare, except, *I'm glad to be home* – and out through the glass doors, Peter striding out in front with the trolley.

'Psst.' Elizabeth felt a tug on her shoulder, followed by Patsy's voice whispering in her ear. 'What about the dress?'

Elizabeth stopped dead and Patsy almost barrelled into her. 'I'm sure it'll be all right. They'll find my bag.' And finally: 'We just need to pray.'

They trundled out of the shadowed hallway, into bright sunshine lighting a big banner that said *Welcome Home Travel Club* in big red letters. And then they were in a mob, all hugging and kissing, and patting Justin on the head and telling him how much he had grown.

'Look pleased to be home, don't they,' said B2 to B1, who had his arm around Di and was dipping his head to kiss her.

'Mmm,' answered B1.

Suddenly, he was grabbed by a woman, he thought her name was Patsy, who gave him a resounding kiss. Pandemonium, he thought, but good sort of pandemonium. Out of the corner of his eye, he caught Katy and Peter in each other's arms. That looked encouraging – but you never knew. Peter was speaking so softly he had to strain to hear.

'I have something for you.'

'Do you?' Katy whispered.

'Would you like it now, it's in my pocket.' He patted his coat pocket.

'What's he got in his pocketses? Is this a riddle?'

'Sort of. It comes with a question.'

'Oh.'

'Should I ask the question here?'

She shut her eyes, drew in a deep breath, and swallowed carefully, 'Maybe.'

The old Peter would have slithered sleekly away, but this was a new man, made resolute by Michael's fatherly wisdom. 'You don't have to answer right now. No pressure.'

Katy noticed that the turmoil around her had subsided and all eyes were glued on their conversation. Rising up from her gut was warmth and fire and a buzz that was making her heart race. It would only take one word from her and the earth would turn on its head. She took another deep breath and out came: 'Try.'

Peter cleared a little space next to the trolley in front of Katy, took her crimson-nailed hand in his, dropped dashingly to one knee. 'My darling Katy,' he said, 'will you be my wife?'

As he knelt there, gazing up into her eyes, she felt the magnetic poles shift and everything stand still. She looked up to clear her head and noticed the circle around her. The three sisters were dripping tears down their lined, grinning faces, Di holding hands with Bob.

Her father was watching Peter with an expression on his face that said he was either going to kiss him or kill him.

Justin – well, Justin had dropped his phone. Welcome to real life Justin, she thought, where happy endings are always possible.

She took a deep breath, looked down into his beautiful blue eyes and time moved on again. 'Of course, I will,' she said, pulling him up into her arms, 'and I hope you're not just marrying me for my marketing strategies.'

Everybody laughed, including Peter as she kissed him.

'You know I am,' he said, coming up for air, 'and your technology skills, and your bookkeeping, and your red hair and your beautiful soul – and because I love you.' He slipped the engagement ring he had bought in the Medieval market in Paris over her finger.

'Me too,' she replied, as the others crowded around to view the ring.

Killing might not be required, thought B2, but I don't think I want to kiss him, and went forward to shake hands with his future son-in-law.

Jeanie Wood

EPILOGUE

'A Christmas weddings,' whispered Elizabeth, 'they're always special.' In her mind's eye was that hot clear day she had walked down this aisle to John, just like this day, it had dawned blue and bright. Where John had once stood, Peter was standing with Bob as his best man and Michael, Justin, Tam, David and Gary as his groomsmen.

'You first,' Patsy said and gave Elizabeth a gentle push.

The yes-woman led the Six Sisters slowly down the aisle of the church one by one. Kathryn reflected that it was a stately step – maestoso – she was thinking as she took her slow pace. She nearly laughed out loud at the next thought – they were all probably going as fast as they could. Walking down was the hard bit, she reasoned, going back they could lean on the men.

Lined up six abreast in front of the holy table, clasping their bouquets, they were resplendent in the maids of honour frocks from the dress shop in the mall. Around their necks the gold hearts gleamed, each stone matching their dresses. The women had said they were hardly maids any more, but Katy declared she didn't care, the sisters were her family and they were all going to be in her wedding party

Carol, sitting on the front seat, was admiring her husband and son in the wedding party and imagining that the Six Sisters were the good fairies, bringing everything a young bride could wish.

There was a hush in the church and all eyes were fixed on Katy, holding firm to her father's arm, treading slowly towards them, a posy of cream roses from Patsy's garden in her hands.

'Oh,' gasped Patsy to Elizabeth, 'she wore it. She wore the dress we bought her in Paris.' Cream lace, it was, fitted to her shapely young body, with pearls around the waltz length hemline. They were remembering standing in the dress store in France, discussing the price, whether she would like it, whether she would wear that colour, whether it was young enough, or long enough, or short enough. Katy had delighted over it when she unwrapped it from the tissue paper, but they had never actually seen her wear it.

Anna smiled at the bright hair under the ancient cream mantilla. Long ago in St. Stephen's cathedral her love had helped her shake it back from her head. She had packed it with her meagre belongings for her own wedding and kept it all those years for someone like a daughter.

Katy reached the front of the church, kissed her father, gave her roses to a shiny-eyed Elizabeth and placed both her hands in Peter's. Here I am, she thought, in my own love story, just as Nanna said I'd be.

Peter was beyond thought. He had gone through rivers of questions and oceans of doubt with Michael on the holiday – and since – and had recently decided to leave it up to God. After all, He seemed to know what He was doing. He took a deep breath, looked into Katy's glistening eyes, smiled – and the world settled into a safe place like an anchor into a riverbed.

Outside the church, after the ceremony, Bill was standing next to Bob.

'Looking forward to a beer, B2?'

'Sure am, B1, can't wait to get out of this clobber and throw one back at Patsy's place.'

'Should be a great party.' Bob smiled.

''Specially since I did up the garden.' Bill winked.

'Reckon they'll make it?' Bob had too much experience with the flip side.

'I sure do, B1, and I reckon you'll be okay, too.' He inclined his head towards the approaching Di, who had her camera at the ready. Bob reddened – must be too hot for him, thought Bill then stifled a laugh – not just the weather.

'Time for photos.' Di gave Bob the camera and then, linking her hands in the crook of each of their elbows, dragged B1 and B2 back to the church porch.

In the mall, local shoppers meandered amongst the tinsel and trees from one store to the next. Which was the best photo, they asked each other?

The Travel Club?

Peter with Katy in her Parisian wedding frock and that gorgeous mantilla?

Bob and Di in Patsy's garden, a toddler swinging ape-like between them?

The family photo with serious Justin?

Justin laid out in front of his travel grandmas?

Hard to pick, they agreed, but they all belong to us.

Peter and Katy lay nestled in each other's arms. 'Happy Christmas, wife,' said Peter

'Yes, it is, husband.' Skin to skin, she could feel his heart beating in time with hers. 'And yes I am.'

'Good. Let's keep it like this.'

'Yes, please.'

'Forever.'

'And ever.'
'Amen.'

Ready for some more adventures?

COMING SOON

THE TRAVEL CLUB RIDES AGAIN

CHAPTER ONE

'They're back,' barked Bill.

'Who?' Bob was staring at his computer, trying valiantly to work in the face of incessant interruption.

B1 and B2, as they were generally known, had been taking care of the Travel Agency while Peter and Katy were on their honeymoon and hopefully enjoying a bit of unaccustomed private time.

Not that anything was ever private around here, thought Bob. From the mall, the butcher, the baker, and *thanks be for electricity*, they didn't have to answer to the candlestick maker – just the hairdresser and all – *yes* – ALL the assistants from the dress shop next door had been constantly asking when their favourite couple would return. Who knew who else might walk in? *Bolt the door,* he wanted to say, but professionalism won out. There was silence. He looked up at Bill who was gesticulating towards the glass shopfront with his head and eyes simultaneously, looking like Skippy the Bush Kangaroo. Bobs mouth curved up as the thought swivelled his gaze. There they were, standing hand in hand, peering through the glass, grinning.

The bosses were back.

Peter's nephew, Justin came barrelling out from the photocopier room, through the agency and between the front doors like a rodeo rider on a brumby. He skidded to a halt in front of Peter and Katy and grabbed them both in a huge group hug. B1 and B2 looked at each other and shook their heads.

'Looks like we can have a day off,' said Bill, his face wreathed in a wrinkled grin at the sight of his daughter, Katy.

'Yup.' Bob was feeling a bit let down and reflecting that part time work meant looking after a toddler - hardly a day off.

The Travel Club sat, cups hot in hand, cake crumbing in mouth, waiting for a story like children at bedtime.

'How was Russia?' asked Patsy.

What Patsy really wanted to say was *how's married life?* But Elizabeth had warned her not to ask personal questions – well not too personal. Patsy was counting on that being a grey area.

'Cold,' replied Peter with a wry smile.

'Beautiful,' Katy added laughing. 'Well both really. Not many people visit Moscow in the dead of winter.'

'What about Napoleon?' Justin put in. The assembly gawked

at him and he looked offended. He nodded at Kathryn. 'I listened to the 1812 Overture like you told me. And I read the story about it.'

She glowed back at him. 'What a good boy,' she mouthed.

'And Hitler,' Bill put in, winking at Patsy. 'Well, he tried to.'

'Neither of them was on their honeymoon.' Patsy pointed out helpfully, grinning back at him.

'*We* managed to keep warm.' Peter stared down into his cup, smiling eyes glittering under the dirty blond curls flopping over his forehead.

Patsy peered at Elizabeth, who pursed her lips and shook her grey curls. No, not allowed to follow up on that comment.

'Most places were well heated.' Peter lifted his head and looked around the group. 'We only needed those puffer coats and boots outside.'

'And hats and gloves.' Katy's eyes were shining like sunlit snow. 'And we took a troika ride in the snow, under the stars, wrapped in furs, shushing along.' Her Nanna's long-remembered words honeyed her mouth, and she sighed. 'Our breath froze on our faces.' Head on one side she smiled longingly at Peter, and they gazed into each other's eyes, lost in that shared joy's secret place.

The communal 'ahhh' around the table eased them back to reality.

Peter jumped into the relative silence. 'We started in St. Petersburg and visited the Hermitage Museum and the Winter Palace. Magnificent. No wonder there was a revolution. All that gold everywhere.'

'Then we toured the Peterhof museum and castle. It was so good,' Katy went on. 'My favourite was the portrait of Catherine the

Great astride a horse in a man's military uniform. She knocked off her incompetent husband to become the Empress of Russia. Good on her. The guide said he died of a heart attack - the sort you get from a sword.'

Peter raised both hands in defeat and declared, 'I'll work harder. Don't kill me.'

Everybody laughed. 'Now that's what I call feminism,' Patsy declared and looked at Kathryn. 'You must take after your namesake.' She winked. 'But you knock 'em dead with your music.' Kathryn gave a wry laugh and raised her carefully outlined eyebrows.

Peter held up a quelling hand. 'We had five days there, wandering around and enjoying all the splendour. Then we caught the Sapsan train to Moscow. That was fantastic.' He looked sideways at Katy, who nodded her agreement. 'It was like a bullet through snowy forests. We were warm and snug in our own compartment.'

Katy added, 'Just like that scene in Dr Zhivago, only warmer and more luxy.'

'How long were you on the train?' asked Justin, caught up in the exoticism of the moment.

'Four hours.'

'Wow,' said Patsy, 'and in your own private compartment.'

Elizabeth narrowed her eyes and pursed her lips, giving her friend the Gorgon stare. Katy started to giggle. Peter, smirked down into his cup. 'Moscow was great,' he said, striking before his wife could speak. 'So much to see. And snow everywhere.'

'Like icing sugar,' interposed Katy, 'and sometimes like ice cream.'

'Cold and wet,' finished Peter, ever the realist. 'Nice to come back to the sun.'

'What was your favourite part of Moscow?' asked Bob

'The train stations,' the couple chorused, then laughed.

'Awesome,' said Katy.

'Bizarre.' Peter screwed up his face. 'They were built as people's palaces with chandeliers and works of art. Full of Stalinist propaganda. And the long deep escalators went at light-speed.'

'Fast trains, flying escalators, and gazillion commuters. Unbelievable!' Katy was butterflying patterns in the air with hands, conveying the difference of the place, the nuance of culture, the lure of the unknown. 'I loved them.' She said simply, looking at Peter as she did, so he blushed, and everybody else felt like outsiders.

'So,' said Peter, 'Tell us what you've been up to.'

ABOUT THE AUTHOR

Jeanie Wood is a mother of four, grandmother to fourteen, music teacher, Scout Leader and writer who lives in Sydney's Western suburbs.

She left school at 16 after the sudden death of her father. With her children grown, she returned to a local high school to sit her HSC, moving on to Macquarie University where she gained First Class honours in English, followed by a PhD in Creative Writing.

She is an active member of her community, teaching ESL in her church, running a Scout Group, and mentoring young scouts and guides in Cumberland Gang Show to write new material for the stage – and still composing the occasional song - and runs her own private music teaching studio.

This is her first novel, and is part of a series based on a wealth of living, the richness of relationships and family, and the excitement of travel.

Made in the USA
Coppell, TX
01 April 2024

30744193R00125